The porch light flickered, casting the area in shadows. She'd been meaning to change that bulb.

"Thanks again," she said, getting her keys out of her purse.

Jacobe took her elbow in his hand and turned her to face him. He stood so close that she had to tilt her head even farther back to meet his gaze. In the flickering light of the porch, she couldn't make out the expression in his eyes.

"I respect your honesty, Danielle." His other hand came up to brush across her chin. "Don't think this kiss means otherwise."

Her heart fluttered and anticipation tingled every inch of skin on her body. "Who said you could kiss me?"

His dark eyes met hers and the corners of his mouth tilted up in a sexy smile. "Tell me I can't and I won't."

The air crackled around them. Sparks of heat filled her chest. Her eyes lowered to his lips. Full and soft. Based on the smoldering heat in his eyes, his lips desperately wanted to touch hers.

"One kiss," she whispered.

Dear Reader,

I'm no sports expert, but since I live in a house with an avid sports fan—my hubby—it's no wonder I got the idea for a sports romance. Once that idea hit, I immediately wanted the story to be a basketball romance. Maybe because my favorite sport in high school was basketball and my first professional-athlete crush was a basketball superstar.

Full Court Seduction is the result of that inspiration. Jacobe Jenkins is a basketball star who needs to improve his reputation. Danielle Stewart is an environmental activist who needs publicity for her cause. They knew each other in college and shared one night neither one of them can forget. They come together for mutual benefit, yet their chemistry is hard to ignore.

Hope you enjoy Jacobe and Danielle's journey to their happily-ever-after.

Sincerely,

Synithia W.

Full
COURT
Seduction

SYNITHIA WILLIAMS

HARLEQUIN® KIMANI™ ROMANCE

Recycling programs
for this product may
not exist in your area.

ISBN-13: 978-0-373-86487-4

Full Court Seduction

Copyright © 2017 by Synithia R. Williams

Printed in U.S.A.

A12006 739232

Synithia Williams has been an avid romance-novel lover since picking up her first at the age of thirteen. It was only natural that she would begin penning her own romances soon after—much to the chagrin of her high school math teachers. She's a native of South Carolina and now writes romances as hot as their southern settings. Outside of writing, she works on water quality and sustainability issues for local government. She's married to her own personal hero, and they have two sons who've convinced her that professional wrestling and superheroes are supreme entertainment. When she isn't working, writing or being a wife and mother, she's usually bingeing on TV series, playing around on social media or planning her next girls' night out with friends. You can learn more about Synithia by visiting her website, www.synithiawilliams.com, where she blogs about writing, life and relationships.

Books by Synithia Williams

Harlequin Kimani Romance

A New York Kind of Love
A Malibu Kind of Romance
Full Court Seduction

For Ashley and Toya, my ride-or-die sisters since forever.

Acknowledgments

The biggest thanks to Farrah Rochon for organizing
the Destin Divas Retreat. I plotted *Full Court Seduction*
at that retreat and made a few new writing friends. I have
to give special thanks to Destin Divas Jamie Wesley,
Carla Freed and Lena Hart for helping me define
a "Hollywood ending" for Jacobe and Danielle,
and divas K. M. Jackson and Kaia Danielle
for your valuable feedback on the draft. Finally,
to my wonderful hubby, I truly appreciate you
watching our two boys while I'm off in the writing world.
Writing would be much harder without your support.

Chapter 1

Event planning would be the death of her.

Which was why Danielle had taken a break from planning the next few events for the St. Johns River Watchers to get a cup of coffee. She was pretty sure that if she hadn't taken the break, her heart was going to wave the white flag and go on permanent strike against the stress she put herself through.

The sound of footsteps running toward the kitchen of the small beachfront cottage that served as the River Watchers office preceded the appearance of Danielle's education-and-outreach coordinator, who was rushing toward the door.

"Danielle, have you heard?" Debra said between huffs. Her cheeks were red from the sprint. She pushed her thin jet-black hair behind her ears, making her gothic-inspired cross earrings swing against her pale neck. Her black pants, boots and *Nightmare Before*

Christmas T-shirt were splattered with glitter, a leftover from a presentation at a kindergarten class earlier today.

"Heard what?"

Debra looked to the ceiling and shook her head. "You're not angry, so I'm assuming you haven't heard. I spoke with Mr. Springfield today—the state hasn't automatically denied the permit allowing Clear Water to discharge into Springfield Creek."

Danielle set the mug on the counter, coffee and gala temporarily forgotten, and crossed to the small wooden dinette table. "What? They should be shutting down, not expanding."

She'd fought on behalf of the River Watchers all last year to get Clear Water's permits revoked. The small wastewater provider couldn't handle the sewage from the rapidly growing area coming to them and had exceeded their permit limits for pollution levels going into a tributary of the river. The state had agreed and ordered Clear Water to come up with a plan to reduce pollution or shut down.

"They think that expanding their operation and adding another discharge point will make them meet our demands."

"The creek can't handle that."

Debra nodded. "I know that. Mr. Springfield certainly doesn't want it going into the creek. He worked too hard with us to put the easements in place that will stop it from future development. Now all those efforts are threatened if this happens."

Danielle's brain buzzed with a variety of ideas. They needed to do something. "We need to get in front of the county commissioners at their next meeting. Get them to deny any permits for the expansion. If this goes through it doesn't just hurt Mr. Springfield, it had the potential to hurt everyone living in the Crescent Acres community."

Crescent Acres was a low-income neighborhood in an area just south of Jacksonville, Florida. Springfield Creek flowed right through the neighborhood before it entered Mr. Springfield's property. Many of the people who lived there fished and played in that creek. If a sewer provider that already couldn't meet their current permit limits started dumping poorly treated wastewater into the creek the effects could be devastating.

"I'm already talking to the commissioner's clerk to see about getting on the agenda," Debra said.

"Any idea what stance the county wants to take?"

Though the county leaders sometimes voted to preserve the areas going into the river, they also rarely took a huge stance on environmental issues.

Debra shook her head. "No idea."

Danielle slapped her fist into her opposite palm. "We've got to get them to fight this."

Debra chuckled. "I think they're already expecting your call. The clerk remembers how much you hounded the state to go after Clear Water last year."

"I only scheduled a small press conference."

Debra smirked. "You put out a rally cry to our supporters to show up in front of the Clear Water gates with old toilets and signs that said 'Poop in the toilet, not our river.'"

Danielle shrugged and smothered a grin. She was pretty proud of that idea. "It got everyone's attention. We'll need something equally big to get people paying attention again. That was just a year ago, but no one is watching what Clear Water is doing now. I can't believe they have the nerve to try and dump into Springfield Creek."

"They'll be ready for battle after you gave them so much grief before."

Danielle had been with the River Watchers since graduating from the University of Miami five years ago. When her sampling efforts proved Clear Water was dumping catastrophic amounts of pollution into the river, she'd spearheaded a movement against the provider. Her actions quickly turned the small organization into the most well-known conservation watchdog in the community. She'd gone from organizing their monitoring program to an executive director in a record five years.

"Does it look like I can't go to battle with them?" Danielle turned, picked up her coffee mug off the counter and took a sip.

"Of course you don't look like you're ready for battle. That's why you win. You surprise people with ferocious tenacity beneath your girl-next-door exterior."

"I do not."

"Yeah. You do." Debra eyed Danielle from head to toe.

Danielle straightened her glasses and smoothed the front of the white cardigan she wore over a navy sundress. "Maybe I use that as a slight tactical advantage."

"You're never afraid to do battle with anyone, which is why I love working with you."

"Don't try and butter me up for a raise," Danielle teased. "I won't be able to cover the part-time salaries of the interns next fiscal year if we can't get any more donors."

"I'm not worried. Since you became executive director a year ago the donations have improved. The idea for the River Gala and silent auction this year was smart. I'm sure that'll help raise some funds."

Debra nodded and looked at Danielle like she was the great black hope. Danielle's earlier freak-out about the success of the events she planned came back full force. They would need several successful events, not just the gala in a few weeks, to keep their doors open.

"If it makes you feel any better," Debra said. "I think Mr. Springfield knows this is going to be a huge battle for us. He gave us a gift to thank us for our efforts."

"A gift?"

"Two tickets...wait let me start over. Two—*court-side*—tickets for tonight's Jacksonville Gators game." Debra pulled the tickets from her back pocket. "He said to go, enjoy and relax before the fight. I know you're a huge fan. I figured you'd be excited."

Danielle rushed over to Debra's side to snatch the tickets. "Are you for real?" She scanned the tickets to confirm the unbelievable news.

"Yep. Mr. Springfield has to go out of town tonight. He said he couldn't think of two more deserving ladies than us."

"Tonight's game is a big one for them. They're playing Miami."

"Ooh, double the eye candy. Miami has some sexy players." She bumped Danielle with her elbow.

"I wasn't thinking about the sex appeal of the players. If this game was after the gala it would've made a great prize for the auction."

Debra poked Danielle's shoulder. "Will you stop thinking about the gala for a second and accept this completely fantastic gift?"

Danielle rubbed her shoulder even though the spot didn't hurt. "I don't always think about work. And we had drinks a few weeks ago."

"Drinks with the other river rats a month ago doesn't

count," Debra said, referring to the other conservation leaders in the area.

They'd gotten the nickname after a snarky reporter accused the environmental community of "scurrying around the river looking for problems" like rats. Instead of getting offended, Danielle insisted they accept the nickname. They did look for problems, and they made sure the problems were fixed.

Some called her overzealous. She didn't care. There wasn't much she could hold on to in her life. She was single, her parents were always busy with other things, she had no siblings, and she hadn't had a significant relationship since college. Her passion for protecting the river was about the only thing to keep her warm at night. A state some would consider depressing if they didn't consider her reasons.

The Ridgeport area was her home. She'd inserted herself in the community, made connections with residents and other activists there. What she did to protect the people hurt by industries like Clear Water, and their appreciation for her efforts, was the only proof she had that she mattered to someone.

"Come on, Danielle. We've got courtside seats. We have to go."

Danielle did a quick count in her head. It had been over a month since she'd done anything remotely fun that had nothing to do with raising money for the River Watchers. "Why not?"

Debra did a quick shimmy of her hips and grinned. "Yay! It's going to be so much fun. Hey, we're right behind the bench. Maybe you can put that unassuming girl-next-door charm on blast and snatch a towel from one of the players."

"Really, Debra, how am I supposed to do that?"

"They won't suspect you of stealing a towel," Debra said with a wiggle of her eyebrows. "Try to go for one that Jacobe Jenkins uses to wipe the sweat from his brow. Since you salivate every time you see him on television or on a billboard."

Danielle waved a dismissive hand, but her heart wasn't so indifferent. It jumped with a secret thrill of excitement. "I do not salivate."

Debra's smirk screamed, *Yeah, right.* "Yeah. You do. You both were at the University of Miami at the same time. Did you drool over him then, too?"

Drooling over Jacobe Jenkins was an understatement. Hiding how much desire gripped her whenever he came near had become her number-one priority. Except for that one night. Danielle tried to force the long-ago encounter from her mind and focus on the myriad of ways Jacobe Jenkins had irritated her, when he wasn't sending her estrogen levels through the roof.

"Every time I was around Jacobe he was being a cocky jock who thought the world was his to command, or he was on his way to a party."

Debra held up both hands in front of her body. "Shut the front door. You did not tell me you know Jacobe Jenkins!"

"I don't *know* Jacobe. I knew him. A hundred years ago when we were freshmen in college. I tutored him a few times in Biology 101. He left for the draft right after freshman year, and I never saw him again. A few brief interactions do not count as *knowing* him."

One night of fast and hot sex the night before the draft could count as knowing him, but Danielle was taking that secret to her grave.

"It's still cool that you kinda know him. It'll be fun to sit right behind him and the rest of the team at the game.

Maybe he'll see you and recognize you. Then he can introduce me to one of his sexy teammates. That team is full of grade-A, prime-choice, hot-guy sexiness."

"First of all, I doubt he'd recognize me. Second, if he did I doubt even more that he'd speak to me. Third, prime-choice, hot-guy sexiness? What is that?"

"Um, every single man on that team."

Debra and Danielle both laughed. Someone cleared their throat. They both stifled the laughter and turned toward the door. One of the female interns who took water samples along the river stood there with a cooler in her hand. "I'm going to take some samples on the beach today. You need anything before I go?"

Danielle shook her head and tried to look professional. Hard to do after being caught talking about prime male sexiness. "No, Marie, we're good."

As soon as the young woman walked away, Danielle bumped Debra. "We've got to stop talking about the men of the Jacksonville Gators like they're pieces of meat. It's not professional in front of the interns."

"The interns drool over those men, too," Debra said, grinning. "So, are you really good to go? Don't you want to see the super-hot men on this team up close?"

A shiver of anticipation raced through Danielle. Seeing Jacobe up close and in person would be fun. Based on media reports, he was cockier and even more arrogant than she remembered. Shortly after joining the league he'd gotten into some trouble for fighting and partying hard. The team that had drafted him had traded him to Jacksonville two years before. Jacksonville had been a laughingstock of the league until Jacobe joined and they picked up a few more free agents and draft picks. Some were even talking play-offs this year. Of course he wouldn't recognize her, but she was a fan of the team, and seeing him again even if from afar would be kind of thrilling.

You seriously need to find a man.

Danielle pushed that thought aside. She didn't need anyone to validate her. She had her work. People moved on. The cause remained the same.

She looked at Debra and nodded. "I'm in."

The Jacksonville arena buzzed with the excitement of the rivalry game. The same energy pumped full throttle through Danielle and Debra. Danielle had only been to two other Gators games. Each time she'd sat in the nosebleed seats. The Gators had almost made it to the play-offs last season, but had lost in overtime. That was the last game she'd come to. She and the rest of the fans had felt the team's disappointment that night. This year they'd played each game as if it were a rematch of that heartbreaking loss. With each win, ticket prices increased. Nosebleed seats were getting to be out of her budget. Courtside had only been a dream before Mr. Springfield's gift.

Debra gripped Danielle's arm. "Oh, my God, there he goes again!"

"Are you going to do that all night," Danielle said, swatting at Debra's hand. Every time Jacobe came anywhere near the bench Debra went into a fit of hormones. They both wore Gators T-shirts and jeans. Debra's proudly included Jacobe's number, 06, on the back. Jacobe wasn't on the bench often. He'd spent most of the first half contributing to his team's six-point lead over Miami. The few times he did come to the bench, Debra's enthusiasm rivaled that of someone who'd just won the Powerball jackpot.

Debra released Danielle's arm. "I can't help it. He's so damn fine."

Danielle couldn't argue with that. Instead, she took stock of Jacobe's fineness herself. And, boy, was that man fine. Six feet and four inches of long, lean muscle, smooth, terra-cotta skin and walnut-colored eyes. He played point guard and led the team with ease and confidence. His large body was a thing of grace and beauty. He handled the ball with self-assurance, ran up and down the court without hesitation and effortlessly faked out the opponent defending him. Since he'd been traded to the Gators she'd seen images of him everywhere, but being this close to him in action proved how inadequate billboards, television commercials and nosebleed seats were at portraying his skill and hotness.

Danielle alternated between greedily studying his powerfully built body and jumping up to cheer with the rest of the fans every time he scored. When she'd first come into the arena she'd considered keeping to her seat to try not to draw any attention to herself. That idea was immediately dropped after she was swept away by the buzz of electricity in the crowd. What did it matter if he did happen to look behind the bench? Jacobe had more than likely forgotten about her. Even if he happened to remember the tutor he'd slept with one night in college, she doubted he thought of her often or remembered much about her.

That night she'd known she would be treated as just another groupie, but knowing that hadn't kept her away. Despite the attraction that sizzled between them, Jacobe had never tried to hook up with her. He'd been dating a girl named Christy, and, unlike many of the jocks she knew, he'd been faithful to her. Getting Jacobe to stray from the girl he'd started dating in high school had been a game for so many girls. A game Danielle had prided herself on staying out of. Then she'd heard that Jacobe and Christy had broken up.

To this day she couldn't believe her audacity, but a switch had gone off in her head after hearing about the breakup. A part of her felt that if he was single she wasn't being just another girl trying to steal him away. The thought of that day crept into her head, dulling the noise of the crowd as she remembered how she'd lit into him for keeping her waiting for another tutoring session.

"Yo, I said I was sorry. I have a party to prepare for," he'd said.

"You know what, go to your party and quit wasting my time," Danielle shot back. *"I've got better things to do than babysit jocks."*

"You know what, I've got better things to do than get lectured by you," he'd said, then turned to his roommate, who'd come with him to the library. *"Come on, man, let's get out of here."*

His roommate had snickered and tapped Jacobe on the arm. "Dude, why don't you two just hit and get it over with? You know all that fighting is just foreplay."

Jacobe's sexy brown eyes had raked over every inch of her body. "I'd love to. She doesn't want to handle all this." He'd given her a cocky smile before turning and leaving.

That one simple statement had made her blood boil, though not from rage. She hadn't known if he was truly interested or just wanted to tease her, but she'd gone to his pre-draft party that night wearing a sexy black dress she'd bought on a whim a month earlier. She'd gotten her answer. He had been interested, and she was able to handle what he offered.

They'd left the room in an awkward silence. Jacobe

had promised to call. She hadn't believed him. The next day he'd flown to New York for the draft, and she'd never heard from him again. Through the grapevine, she'd learned he'd reconnected with Christy.

She didn't regret their time together. Over time she'd gotten over him never calling. She'd gone over there to discover if he'd felt the same attraction she'd spent the year trying to ignore, and she'd gotten her answer.

The buzzer for the end of the second quarter sounded. Danielle jerked out of the past. Debra was too busy cheering to notice Danielle was distracted. The crowd clapped as the Gators ran off the court. Danielle joined in. Jacobe walked over to the chair right in front of where Danielle stood, snatched up a towel and wiped his face.

He looked up into the crowd, spread his arms wide and waved them up and down. "This is our house!" he yelled, getting the crowd hyped even more. His intensity burned off him in waves.

A tiny shiver ran through her. His gaze lowered from the upper stands and landed right on hers. Most of the air evacuated her lungs. He held her gaze barely a second before looking away.

He took a step, paused, frowned and then turned to stare directly at her again.

Danielle's heart thudded, and the remaining air in her lungs dissolved like cheap tissue paper. Her stomach clenched right before a thousand feathers tickled her inside. His eyes lightened, maybe with recognition—she couldn't tell—but the smile that spread his lips sent a bolt of lightning straight to her core.

Then he turned and walked with the rest of the team into the locker room. Danielle stood there, stupefied. Had the moment happened, or had she just imagined that? He couldn't possibly remember her, could he? No, not after all these years.

"Danielle, what was that?" Debra's excited voice zipped Danielle to the present.

"What was what?"

"He looked at you, and he looked happy to see you."

Danielle pushed her glasses farther up her nose and shook her head. "No, he looked into the crowd. He wasn't looking at me."

"I saw the look."

"Forget the look. The look means nothing." She was going to make it mean nothing anyway. "Let's go to the concession stand. I want some popcorn."

The lines were so long that the trek for popcorn and sodas took most of halftime. By the time they made their way back to the seats, the teams were running onto the court to warm up. Danielle staunchly avoided watching Jacobe. She may have enjoyed that second of eye contact, but that didn't mean she had to visually stalk him for the rest of the night.

Debra chocked on her popcorn and grabbed Danielle's arm. "He's coming over."

No need to pretend she didn't know who she was talking about. "His chair is right in front of us."

"No, he's looking at you and coming this way."

"Will you stop it, Jacobe Jenkins isn't—"

"Danielle?" A male voice that didn't sound quite sure if he was getting her name right interrupted.

Danielle's hands became slick. Her heart fluttered like a hummingbird's wings against her ribs. *Oh, wow. It was him.*

She slowly pivoted in her chair to look into a pair of sexy brown eyes. He smiled at her with a hint of unsureness in his gaze.

"Oh…hi, Jacobe."

"Danielle Stewart…right?"

She nodded. "That's me."

"What are you doing here?"

"Enjoying the game."

He laughed. "Yeah, I guess so. What have you been up to?"

Danielle glanced around. Some of the courtside reporters were looking their way. A few even snapped some pictures. Danielle squirmed self-consciously in her seat. "I work for the St. Johns River Watchers."

"You live around here?" Sweat ran down his face, to his neck and into the jersey covering his wide, muscled torso.

Why in the world was a sweaty man so damn sexy? "Yep."

He ran the towel over his face, thankfully removing the distracting sweat. Unfortunately, the movement brought attention to his fantastically sculpted arms. "This your first game?"

"No. My first courtside seat, though."

He nodded. "Cool. What are you doing after the game?"

She blinked, thrown off by the question. "Going home."

He shook his head, dismissing her statement. "The guys from the team usually meet up at a pool bar downtown called The Hall. Meet me there after the game."

Debra's leg bounced like a supercharged Chihuahua in Danielle's periphery. "The Hall?" Had her voice really just squeaked? She cleared her throat.

"Yeah. You know where it is? They're usually selective about letting people in after a home game because the team hangs out there afterward, but I'll call ahead and tell them you're cool. Come by. Let's catch up."

One of his teammates called. Jacobe looked over his

Chapter 2

Typically, when Jacobe entered The Hall after a game and heard the drum of old-school hip-hop and smelled the Buffalo wings the place was known for, he was instantly ready to party. Tonight, the tension that had taken over his neck and shoulders since he'd knocked out Rob Jackson wouldn't go away. He shouldn't have done that. The league would probably suspend him for that. Not what he needed right before the play-offs. Taking the Gators to the play-offs would secure his place as one of the best players in the league, which was something he knew, but the trouble in his past kept others from admitting it. It would also make the final argument for him to be signed by Phoenix next year. They were building a superteam, and Jacobe was aiming to be on that team.

He could see the years of winning the finals in his future if that happened. The chance was now a big if. His agent had already called and told him not to talk to shoulder to acknowledge him, then looked back at her. "I'll see you there later." Not a question.

She was too stunned to get angry at his direction or think of an excuse to say no. "Um...yeah. Sure, we'll stop by."

He grinned. "Cool." He spun and rejoined the team.

Debra leaned in. Danielle lifted her hand to stop her from saying anything. "Stop. The reporters are still watching. Save the gushing for after the game."

"Fine, but there will be tons of gushing in the car."

Danielle nodded and took a sip from her soda. She had to keep her composure for the reporters still looking her way. She knew they had to be wondering who she was.

For the entire third quarter, she replayed the conversation and wondered what it meant. He'd seemed almost happy to see her. Happy? Had he thought of her over the years? Maybe she'd jumped the gun in assuming he could so easily forget her and move on. Maybe Jacobe wasn't as self-centered as she remembered. Maybe the whole bad-boy persona that the media portrayed was just that—a persona.

All those maybes floated away when, halfway through the fourth quarter, Jacobe pushed a referee aside so he could deliver a right hook to an opposing player and left the guy knocked out cold on the floor. He smirked, then stepped over the downed opponent. Danielle sighed and shook her head. Apparently, Jacobe was still the arrogant, cocky jock she'd taken him for.

any reporters while he tried to smooth things out with managers of both teams.

He shouldn't have hit Rob, but he damn sure didn't regret it. *How's your son? Oh, wait, you don't have a son.*

Rob had tossed out the low blow right before Jacobe knocked him out. Jacobe kept his private life private, but Rob had been his teammate four years ago when Jacobe had learned that the woman he'd dated since high school had played him for a fool.

Tossing aside thoughts of Rob, suspension and the worst mistake of his life—Christy—Jacobe scanned the crowded room. After home games The Hall was typically brimming with people. The team came there to play pool and celebrate after a win and the locals had figured that out. The high-top tables were filled with people, along with the chrome stools around the bar. There were people at the pool tables that lined the room, as well, except for the empty table at the end. That's where the Gators played.

His search wasn't just to check out the crowd. He looked for one person in particular. It wasn't long before his gaze landed on Danielle Stewart and the friend she'd been with at the game, sitting at the end of the bar sipping on fruity-looking drinks. His tension eased.

Danielle Stewart. Just thinking of her brought a smile to his lips. His prim-and-proper tutor who had lectured him about the importance of recycling and saving the planet while simultaneously giving him a raging hard-on. If it weren't for that one night in college, he never would have believed she'd felt any of the attraction that always bubbled up in him like molten lava when she was around.

"That's the girl from the game, right?" His teammate Kevin Kouky asked from his right. At six foot seven, Kevin was taller than Jacobe's six-four. His golden-brown skin was hidden behind a myriad of tattoos and one-inch plugs filled his ears.

"That's the girl," Isaiah Reynolds, another teammate, said from his left. Where Kevin's appearance made old ladies cross the street when they saw him coming, Isaiah made them smile and want to pinch his cheeks. He and Jacobe were the same height, but the similarity ended there. Isaiah had "boy you could take home to mama" down pat with his prim-and-proper attire, right down to his signature bow ties.

Will Hampton nodded and grinned. "That's the girl alright." The mischief in Will's eyes sparkled brighter than the diamonds in his ears. The shortest of the group at six one, Will was also the jokester of the team.

Jacobe hadn't called any man a friend in years. Outside of accepting the mentorship of movie star Irvin Freeman and singer Dante Wilson, Jacobe kept most people at arm's length. History had taught him that. Away from the stadium, the only people he preferred hanging with were Kevin, Isaiah, and Will. They were cool, though he still wasn't sure if he could trust them.

"Her name is Danielle," he said. "We knew each other in college. I haven't seen her since the night before the draft."

Kevin bumped him with his elbow. "You seemed pretty happy to see her."

Jacobe shrugged. He had been surprised to see her. Pleasantly surprised. After Christy's betrayal he'd often wondered what would have happened if he'd called Danielle again. "I wouldn't mind reconnecting."

Especially in the bedroom. He didn't know what bit of fate had put Danielle in the courtside seats behind the bench tonight, but he had no intention of squandering the good fortune. He'd love nothing more than a repeat of their night together.

Danielle and her friend stopped their conversation to look their way. Her eyes widened behind those cute black-and-gold glasses she wore before she turned toward her friend. The dark-haired woman elbowed Danielle and said something. Danielle looked back his way and gave him a shy smile.

Ah, yeah, he was going to thoroughly enjoy reconnecting with Danielle Stewart. She'd driven him crazy back then, pestering him to use his popularity for good. The only person who'd seemed to think he could be good at something other than playing ball.

Her lectures had always fallen on deaf ears. Mainly because he couldn't stop himself from thinking of peeling off those cute little cardigan sweaters she seemed to always wear and kissing her until the passion in her warm dark eyes was because of him instead of whatever cause she was championing. He'd always wondered what she would do if she'd known that while she droned on about ecosystems or some other nonsense, he'd wanted nothing more than to plop her on top of the nearest desk and make her glasses fog up.

He lifted his head in acknowledgment, then crossed the room her way. Isaiah, Kevin and Will followed. People stopped and congratulated him and the guys on the win. He spoke, but kept his attention on Danielle. She wore a fitted gold-colored Jacksonville Gators T-shirt that made her luscious breasts look like twin works of art, ankle-length jeans that hugged her ass perfectly and flats. Her thick, dark, shoulder-length hair was parted on the side to sweetly frame her heart-shaped face.

"You came," he said when he got to her side. He

opened his arms and leaned in for a hug. He had to hug her. She was too cute and curvy to not hug.

Her eyes widened, but she leaned in from the waist and patted his back. Jacobe fought the urge to pull her in for a real hug instead of one that left enough space for two small kids to run through.

"Well, you invited me." Her eyes met his and she sucked in a breath, then looked away. "This is my co-worker, Debra." She straightened her glasses and gave another shy smile.

She was still attracted to him. Good, because if she'd shown up with any intentions of reliving their night together he was game. He needed a distraction. They'd won, but the price he'd have to pay for hitting Rob hovered over him like a cloud.

He reached out a hand to the pretty woman next to Danielle. "Nice to meet you, Debra. I'm Jacobe. These guys here are my teammates, Kevin, Isaiah and Will. Fellas, this is Danielle Stewart."

The guys nodded and shook the ladies' hands. Jacobe watched both of them for any signs that they were interested in Danielle. Interest did light up their eyes, but mainly in the way they darted glances between Jacobe and Danielle. He hoped his instincts were right. He didn't need another teammate sleeping with the same chick as him. He had definite plans to eventually sleep with Danielle again.

Debra grinned and shook his head. "I know who all of you are. We're both big fans."

Jacobe looked back at Danielle. "You're a fan?"

She nodded and met his eye without glancing away like she had before. "I am."

"How long have you been in Jacksonville?"

"Since right after college."

Jacobe frowned, upset by the idea that she'd been so close without him even knowing. Though he had thought of her over the years, he hadn't gone so far as to track her down. "I didn't know that."

"We don't exactly hang out in the same circles." She glanced at his teammates.

"I guess not."

Debra leaned forward. "So, Jacobe, how do you know Danielle?"

Jacobe met Debra's eyes and searched for any indication she already knew about his one night with Danielle. He couldn't fault Danielle for telling people about that night—a few of the women he'd had one-night stands with over the years had loved to brag about it afterward. He would be slightly disappointed if Danielle had done the same. That night had been spontaneous and wonderful, awkward but somehow special. A secret between them. He'd never expected her to brag.

"What did Danielle say?"

"That she helped you study, but that's about it."

Relief eased more of the tension. She hadn't bragged to her friend. "Danielle tried helping me out in biology. I was a little hardheaded then."

Danielle raised a brow. "Just a little."

Debra leaned forward and looked expectantly between him and Danielle. "Was she just as driven back then as she is now?"

"When it came to biology and giving back she was. I remember her always trying to get me to volunteer for various causes or skip parties to study."

Danielle smirked and leaned against the bar. "Tried but was unsuccessful. You never wanted to volunteer, and there was always some party to attend."

"I gave back in my own way. You always liked to judge."

Her shoulders straightened. "I didn't judge."

"Yes, you did." He looked back at Debra. "When she rolled up the sleeves of those cute little sweaters she wore I knew she was pissed and that someone was about to get chewed out."

Debra laughed. "She still does that. In the office we say she's ready for battle."

Danielle held up her hands. "I'm going up against politicians and businessmen. I have to be ready for battle." The familiar fight-for-what's-right tone came to her voice.

Isaiah watched her with growing interest. "Politicians and business men? What do you do?"

"I'm the executive director for the St. Johns River Watchers."

Jacobe exchanged glances with the fellas to see if they recognized the organization's name. Isaiah nodded. Of course he would know. Kevin and Will shrugged.

"Impressive," Isaiah said.

"The River Watchers?" Jacobe asked. "What's that?"

Her look said she was disappointed but not surprised by his ignorance. "We're a watchdog organization that makes sure businesses, governments and citizens aren't doing anything to harm the river. Our goal is to protect the river and, ultimately, the beach."

Jacobe wasn't surprised by her career path. "You're still trying to save the world, huh."

Her shoulders stiffened. "And you're still turning your nose up at saving the world."

Kevin cleared his throat. "Oh, look, I think I see the sign to get out of the cross fire." He looked at Isaiah, Will, and Debra. "Pool, anyone?"

The others agreed quickly and scuttled away. "Wow," Danielle said, watching the four leave. "We still know how to clear a room." She took a sip from the straw in her fruity drink.

Jacobe chuckled. "We didn't even have to raise our voices this time. Remember when they kicked us out of the library?"

She smiled. "Yes, the study session before our first test of the semester. You were so distracted and you kept pulling out your cell phone to do other things."

"The test right before a rivalry game," he replied. "I was trying to watch videos of the other team's footage."

"You couldn't wait until we'd finished? One hour, that's all we had."

"I couldn't help it. We met right after practice. I had basketball on the brain."

"How hard was it to focus for an hour?"

"Very." He thought of that day. Basketball hadn't been the only thing on his brain. "You had on that pink sweater with a tight white T-shirt under it." She'd buttoned the sweater to right beneath her breasts. The swell of her chest above it was like a beacon to his eyes. "I had to look at videos on my phone or stare and wonder how you'd squeezed into that shirt."

Her mouth snapped shut and her eyes were wide. He chuckled. "Yes, I was checking you out back then. I thought you would have figured that out by now."

"I hadn't. I thought it was just that night."

He shook his head. "I wanted you long before that night."

She tucked her hair behind her ears and stared into her drink. "You never said anything."

"I'm not into cheating. Too much drama." Something he'd learned the hard way.

Her eyes flew to his. "Neither am I. I only…did what I did because I'd heard you and Christy broke up."

"We had." They should have stayed broken up.

"But then I heard you two were back together."

"We got back after the draft. She said she was pregnant." He couldn't stop the anger from creeping into his voice.

Her eyes widened. "You have a kid?"

He shook his head. "Thought I did. Turns out he wasn't mine."

"Oh."

"That's why I hit Rob tonight. He brought it up."

She scowled. "In the middle of the game. That's a dick move."

Jacobe grinned. He'd always loved her candor. Her spark. "Some would say the same about me hitting him."

Her brows pulled together and she drew her lower lip between her teeth. "I'd thought that when you hit him and walked away so coldly. I guess I understand now. I'm sorry to hear about what Christy did."

"I don't want to talk about that." He shouldn't have told her. Only a few people knew about that situation. A part of him didn't want Danielle to think he'd slept with her that night and gotten back with Christy on a whim.

He needed to change the subject before the old familiar bitterness of that situation took a hold of him. He'd come here for a distraction. He let his gaze slowly roam over every inch of Danielle's sexy curves. "Instead of talking about the past, how about we get out of here?"

The sympathy in her eyes evaporated. "Excuse me?"

"I thought we could catch up. It's been years."

"Yeah, and we can catch up right here, right now."

"You don't have to be shy with me, Danielle. You popped up at my game, in the seat right behind me. Kind of reminds me of that night. I'm good with us hooking up again."

Danielle leaned back. "I was there because one of our donors gave us his courtside seats. I didn't think you'd even remember or recognize me."

"Why wouldn't I?"

"Because I never heard from you again after that night in college."

"That was my mistake. Believe me."

A vision of Christy in his hotel room after the draft, crying and saying they belonged together and that she was pregnant, popped into his mind. She'd dropped a positive pregnancy test on the bed when he'd accused her of showing up just because he'd been drafted. Would Danielle understand the sense of responsibility that had come over him when he'd seen that plus sign and Christy's tears? That nothing else had mattered other than being a better father than the one he'd had.

"You know you're just the same as you always were." Danielle broke into his thoughts.

He met her gaze, was surprised to see anger in her eyes. "Excuse me?"

"I came here because you invited me. I thought that maybe, despite that night together, you would be cool and decent. That we could... I don't know, talk like the adults we are. I didn't come here so you could try and sleaze your way into my bed." She hopped down from the stool. "You have a good night."

He watched her storm off. She said a few quick words to Debra, who glared at Jacobe before she dropped her pool stick and followed Danielle to the door. Kevin, Isaiah, and Will gave him confused looks. Jacobe cursed and rubbed the bridge of his nose. Damn. Now he'd have to go down to that River Watcher place and apologize for being a jerk.

Jacobe's shoulders were tense as he entered the main conference room for the Gators with his agent, Eric Jones. Eric had caught a red eye flight from Los Angeles to be here for this early morning meeting. Eric would probably be the only one who had Jacobe's back today.

Meetings with the management staff were never fun. He had a pretty good idea of the lecture he was about to receive. *Tone down the aggression. We can't afford to lose you right before the play-offs. Try and keep your name out of the headlines.* He'd heard the same lines constantly over the past few years. Never mind that he had toned down his behavior recently. The situation with Christy was a blow he hadn't known how to handle. He'd taken out his aggression on and off the court. For the most part, he considered himself over that blow. It was only when assholes like Rob used the situation against him on the court that his efforts to stay out of trouble were forgotten.

Three people sat around the conference table. Coach Simpson in the usual polo shirt and khakis he wore on off days. His teal-gray eyes met Jacobe's with determination. Rebecca Force, the team's public relations supervisor, sat primly next to the coach. Brian McClain, one of the team's owners, was the last person at the table. Jacobe's shoulders tightened even more. Brian reminded Jacobe of his high school principal with his graying brown hair, stiff suits and perpetual frown. Like his high school principal, Brian never saw anything good in Jacobe off the basketball court and made no qualms about his opinion that Jacobe joining the team would be a distraction. Only their joint goal of a play-off win for the Gators kept them civil toward each other.

"Are we waiting on anyone else?" Eric asked, after they greeted everyone and sat in the chairs to Coach Simpson's left.

Rebecca shook her head. "No, just waiting on you two."

"Sorry for keeping you all waiting," Jacobe said.

Rebecca gave him what he guessed was supposed to be a friendly smile. The tightness around her eyes contradicted the action. "You're actually right on time. We met for a few minutes before you got here to discuss a few things."

The hairs on the back of his neck stood up. "Let me guess—you met early to talk about me."

Eric held up a hand. "Wait a second, Jacobe. Before you get upset, let's hear what she has to say. Though I would have liked to have been included in any discussions regarding my client."

Jacobe would have liked that too. He looked at Rebecca. "What do you have to say?" He didn't bother to hide his frustration.

He didn't like being *discussed* beforehand like he was a threat that needed to be neutralized. Never had. Not when he was sent to the principal's office in school, or when his mom used to get on the phone with her girlfriends and discuss the latest note sent home from school and all the reasons Jacobe couldn't be well behaved like other kids.

Rebecca broke into his thoughts. "The league commissioner called this morning."

Jacobe scoffed. "Already? I guess he couldn't wait to tell me I've messed up. So what is it? A fine? One-game suspension?"

Eric glared at Jacobe. "Let me do the talking."

Brian jerked forward in his chair. "Try a five-game suspension."

The words stunned Jacobe into temporary silence. "Five games?" He'd expected to miss a game, maybe two, not five. They were a few weeks away from the play-offs. If the team lost at this time they could miss their chance at being a number-one seed. Worse, they may not make it at all.

"Yes. Five," Brian said. "Your antics are hurting the team. When the rest of the owners overrode me and brought you here, I knew it would be a problem. You don't care about this team. You don't care about anyone but yourself."

"I care about the team." The words were automatic. Programmed. Though the guys on the team had grown closer to him than any other teammates he'd had since college, he cared mostly about making his way to the play-offs and, ultimately, Phoenix.

"Of course he cares about the team," Eric said. "He's done everything to dedicate himself to the team."

"If he cared about the team he wouldn't have knocked Rob out."

"Rob deserved a lot more than being knocked out."

Coach sighed and leaned his forearms on the table. "What did he say that set you off?"

"Something he shouldn't have."

Brian scoffed and tossed his hand toward Jacobe. "See, utter lack of caring about the consequences of your actions."

Eric held up his hands. "Look, he gets why he shouldn't have hit him during the game."

"After would be better?" Brian asked.

After the game Jacobe wouldn't have hit him just

once, but that was beside the point. "I shouldn't have let my temper get the better of me. I want to take the team to the play-offs just as much as you want to get us there."

Brian didn't reply. He just sat back in his seat and crossed his arms. He might hate Jacobe, but they both wanted wins.

Rebecca glanced between Jacobe and Brian. When Brian didn't say any more, she focused on Jacobe. "Your popularity with the team's fans is high, but last night there was a lot of chatter on the internet about how you're not good for the team."

"You're winning," Eric said with a grin. "They'll get over it."

She lifted a hand. "That may be true, but Jacobe will be gone for five games. If the team starts to lose, then it'll be easy to blame your hot temper and lack of focus for the losses."

"If you're telling me to play nice, I hear you. No more fighting on the court."

Rebecca shook her head. "We need more than that."

"What?"

"We need a plan. Today."

Eric looked around the table. "You can't be serious?"

Coach Simpson nodded. "We are. We want Jacobe to remain a Gator, that's no secret. We also want *everyone* to see that he's an asset to the team." Coach tilted his head slightly in Brian's direction. The hairs on the back of Jacobe's neck twitched some more. He eventually wanted to go to Phoenix, but if that didn't pan out he didn't need the Gators refusing to sign him next year.

"We've finally hit our rhythm as a team," Coach continued. "If we keep playing like we're playing we've got a shot at the play-offs and, I believe, the title. We've built something great here. Let's keep it going."

"I hear you, Coach, but I can't play if I know every time I foul someone I'm going to be called into the conference room and told to behave."

Brian snorted. "That was a lot more than a foul."

Rebecca cut in before Jacobe could respond. "That's why we met before you were here. We *all* want you to remain a Gator next year."

Jacobe narrowed his eyes and studied them. Coach and Rebecca eyed him intensely, and Brian looked like he was tired of the entire fiasco. Wariness had his stomach churning.

Eric shifted in his seat. "You keep saying that. Are there plans to drop him?"

Rebecca and Coach both shook their heads and said simultaneously, "You know we want him."

Brian sat forward and nailed Jacobe with a hard stare. "You're a free agent next year. We won't keep a liability."

"Are you threatening my client?" Eric's voice turned hard.

Rebecca tried again for the friendly smile. "Of course not. Which is why I'm working on a plan to make you more likable."

Jacobe's shoulders tightened. "Excuse me?"

"You aren't seen out and about doing things in the community. If you take up a project or a cause, people will see that you're giving back instead of just…"

"Being a distraction and hindrance," Jacobe finished for her.

He gritted his teeth. Like many other athletes, Jacobe gave to various charitable organizations. Mostly to programs that mentored young boys and gave them direction and support. He gave his money but not his time. He was still getting his own life figured out—how could he possibly make a good mentor?

Eric gave him a reassuring look before turning to Rebecca. "What are you thinking?"

"We've come up with a list of organizations that you can be seen with."

Jacobe shook his head. This was his image problem. He'd find a way to fix it. "I've already got an idea."

Rebecca frowned. "You do?"

"How about protecting the river," Jacobe said. "It's a big part of our city. I've got a friend who works to protect the St. Johns River and the beach. You can't deny that seeing me out there saving sea turtles or some stuff like that would make people *like* me."

Eric nodded and tapped his finger on the table. "That could work. Being green is in right now."

He almost laughed. He'd known Danielle back when saving the planet wasn't just a fad and she was the earth's number-one champion. "I know it'll work."

"Can you set up something with them by the end of the week?"

"I'm sure I can." He already planned to see Danielle later that day to apologize. He still wanted to sleep with her, but he wouldn't assume she would readily fall into his bed. That night in college was a once-in-a-lifetime action. He had a feeling that the woman she was today wasn't going to come to him on a spontaneous whim. He'd have to earn a place in her bed.

Chapter 3

"I'm sorry, Danielle, but I don't think the River Watchers should push council to oppose Clear Water's expansion."

Danielle fought to keep calm as she stared at the board president. Liberty Meyer was only on the board as an attempt to prove the River Watchers were open to voices from all sides. After Danielle had gone for Clear Water and a few other industries like a pit bull on crack, some in the business community had accused the River Watchers of being too biased. Liberty was a vocal member of the manufacturers' alliance and the River Watchers' attempt to bring the business community in on the discussions. Much to Danielle's chagrin, Liberty ran and won a seat on county council after being assigned to the board. Making her a double pain on Danielle's backside.

"Our organization serves as champions to our natural

resources," Danielle said in a surprisingly calm voice. "If they're allowed to expand and dump into Springfield Creek it'll be devastating to the local ecosystem. Not to mention the neighborhood downstream that uses the creek for fishing and recreation."

"Clear Water expanding will bring jobs," Liberty countered. "If we don't bring jobs, that can be detrimental to the population. I care about the flowers and the fish and birds as much as everyone sitting around this table."

Danielle barely stopped herself from snorting.

"But I care more about the men, women and *children* that rely on me as a member of the county council to keep our economy strong and vital."

"I care about the people here, too. This isn't just about the birds and the flowers, Liberty. Clear Water can't meet their permit limits. There's an entire population who'll be swimming in sewage if they dump into the creek."

Liberty rolled her eyes and waved a hand. "Oh, Danielle, please. That's why we have engineers who can design and build a system that can properly treat the waste. People won't be in sewage. This is why I've always said you're too biased when it comes to these types of decisions."

Debra's hand gripped Danielle's leg beneath the table. The movement effectively stopped Danielle from pouncing onto Liberty. That wasn't the first time the woman had thrown out the comment. Danielle and Debra both believed Liberty was trying to make a case with the board to remove Danielle as director.

Mr. Springfield, who'd watched the exchange silently with the rest of the board members, rapped his knuckles on the table. "Ladies, ladies, you both make very good points. Since I'm directly affected by the expansion, I have to defer from voting, but I think this is important enough for the board to take both sides into consideration. If Clear Water can truly improve by expanding, it's better than having a poorly run system out there. If they cannot, then none of us here want them discharging into Springfield Creek. Let's take a little more time, talk to the people in Environmental Protection and see if Clear Water will come to a board meeting to discuss their plans."

There was a round of agreement at the table. Danielle and Liberty gave tight smiles and stiff nods. Mr. Springfield had made a valid point, though Danielle doubted Clear Water would be willing to come to the table and speak to them.

Danielle nodded. "I'll make the necessary contacts. I'll also speak with the Environmental Protection again and send my findings to the board."

Liberty sat forward and crossed her arms on the table. "Don't spend too much time on that. Remember the gala is the most important thing right now."

Danielle took a slow deep breath before responding. "The plans for the gala are coming along very well. We've got several sponsors." Five. "And ticket sales are promising." Two sold today bringing them to a total of twenty.

"Really? I thought it would be slow considering the lack of promotion."

Debra grabbed Danielle's leg again. The limited promotion was due to the budget cuts on the advertisement. Budget cuts Liberty recommended. "We've been lucky to have been picked up a media sponsor." The local free newspaper counted.

Liberty's smile was fake and tight. "That's good. I

don't know how we'll keep things going as is if we don't bring in more funding."

Translation: make the gala a success or else Liberty had a good reason for Danielle's dismissal.

The meeting ended soon after. Danielle was too annoyed and wound up to sit in her office and work on the final preparations for the river cleanup that weekend.

Debra poked her head in Danielle's door. "Hey, I'm about to go pick up supplies for that school presentation later in the week. You need anything?"

"A hundred ticket sales," Danielle said.

"Don't let Liberty get to you. Sales always start slow. They'll pick up."

Danielle pushed aside her frustration with Liberty. She would make this gala a success. "I know they will." She filled her voice with confidence.

"Hey, I've got something to get your mind off of Liberty. Let's call the rest of the river rats and hang out tonight. Maybe we'll come up with some good ideas to shut up Liberty."

Danielle's first impulse was to say no. She'd rather figure out how to get more ticket sales for the gala. Maybe even do some door knocking for sponsors. But if she thought about it too much she'd go crazy. A night out with people who understood would help. "Set it up."

Debra clapped her hands. "Great! Look I've got to go. Most of the interns are out taking samples. We all have our cells if you need anything."

Danielle smiled and waved at Debra as she floated out of the office. With no one there to help distract her from the fact that Liberty wanted her gone, Danielle opted for the best thing to get her mind off of the uncontrollable things in her life. Kicking off her kitten heels, she slipped on a pair of rain boots and stomped out the back of the cottage and down to the beach. Having an office right on the very water body they were trying to protect was the best thing about her job. Every time she thought her work was getting nowhere or that no one was listening or cared, she could look out her window and see the sun reflecting off the waves and remember what she was fighting for. The one thing that she could hold on to in her life.

It was cloudy and drizzling, so she'd put on her pink North Face raincoat for the walk. She liked the beach when it was sunny, but loved it on drizzly days like today. Not as hot, less crowded, and the waters were choppy due to the winds. The sound of each pounding wave would slowly knock away whatever frustration tightened her muscles.

She'd walked a mile down the beach and was on her way back when her cell phone rang in her jacket pocket. She stopped and pulled it. One look at the screen and the tension that had just drained from her shoulders slowly started back.

"Hi, Mom," she said.

"Hello, Danielle, how are things going with my favorite daughter?" Adele Stewart asked in her cheery voice.

She was an only child, so the compliment didn't give Danielle any false sense of importance. "The board meeting was rough this morning. I'm out walking the beach now."

"Is this about the Clear Water expansion?"

"How did you know about that?"

"I read the board meeting agendas that you send me," Adele said, as if Danielle should have known that.

As little attention as her parents gave her, she was surprised to know that her mom read them. The young girl who still wanted their attention was the part of her that added them to the River Watchers mailing list in the vain hope that they'd at least find her work interesting.

"That's it, actually. I've got a board member who doesn't think we should ask the town to oppose the expansion before the permit is on notice. I disagree."

Adele sighed and Danielle pictured her mom shaking her head in disbelief. "I can't fathom why everyone doesn't understand the important role we play in making this world a better place."

"Not everyone thinks that way."

"They should. Don't worry, honey, good always triumphs over evil."

Danielle chuckled. "She's not evil. She just has her own self-interests."

"People who refuse to take responsibility for improving the world are a form of evil."

Words Danielle had heard most of her life. She loved her parents, but many times she'd wished they'd stopped trying so hard to save everyone else in the world and just focus on raising her.

"Where's Dad?"

"Oh, that's why I called. We're taking in another foster child—a boy, eight years old. His mother is in prison and the his father died last year."

"Another? You've already got two kids."

"I know, but I was so moved by his story when I went to the latest CASA meeting. Danielle, there are so many kids out there who need love. It's our duty to do what we can."

"I know, Mom, but you and Dad don't have to take in every child you come across. I thought you were coming to Ridgeport for the river cleanup this weekend. That'll be hard to do with a new kid in the house."

"Oh, Danielle, don't be selfish. We'll try to make it if we can."

Danielle bit her lower lip and dug the toe of her boot into the wet sand. Adele was an expert at hitting Danielle with the guilty stick. Danielle knew there were kids who needed love and affection. She knew that everyone wasn't blessed to have two parents like she did. But all her life her parents were busy with the causes they took up after they couldn't have another child.

"We don't need our own child. Not when there are so many out there we can shower with love."

Her dad has spoken those words to her mom when she'd cried after another failed pregnancy. Danielle had been nine when she overheard them. A few months later the various projects started. They'd built houses, feed the poor, championed animal rights, and now were taking in foster kids. They had taught her the importance of serving, but they'd also been too busy with their projects to give her any attention. From bad days at school, fights with her friends, or a choral recital they couldn't attend, their comments were always the same. There were people out there who had it worse than her.

Danielle used to wonder why they didn't want to shower their attention on her. Was she not good enough? Even though she was older, the feelings of not being enough for her parents hadn't gone away.

"I'm sorry, Mom," she said. "Bring him along. I've got to meet my new brother sooner or later."

"We'll see what the courts say," Adele said dismissively. "Even though his mother is in jail, they may grant visitation. You know I like to make sure the kids see their parents on weekends if they can."

She had her answer: her parents weren't coming. Eventually, she'd stop caring when they missed something of hers because of another commitment. "Don't worry about it. As long as you guys make the gala in a few weeks that's all that matters. It's the inaugural event. I need to make an impression. It would mean a lot to me if you two were there."

"Of course, dear. Oh, your dad's home. We've got to go get a few things for your brother's room. I'll give you a call later, okay? Love you. Bye."

The call ended before Danielle could say anything more. Danielle stared at the phone for a few seconds, sighed, and then shoved it into her pocket.

"Good thing I don't crave my parents' attention," she said to the wind. "I would be constantly disappointed."

The sounds of excited conversation filtered from the house as Danielle trudged up the steps to the office's back door. She left her rain boots in the mudroom, slipped on her heels and followed the sounds of conversation toward the kitchen. Halfway there, the deeper sound of a man's familiar voice slowed her steps. Her pulse raced with anticipation and she carefully eased her way to the open door.

"Jacobe?" she said.

He stood next to the sink, a mug of coffee in his hand, surrounded by three of the interns. Blue-gray slacks covered his long legs and a crisp white shirt wrapped his muscles like the most desirable of Christmas presents. Unwrapping all of that toned, tight body would be something worth celebrating. He glanced up from the group and hit her with his devastating smile.

"Just the woman I was looking for."

He sounded happy to see her. Heat flooded her cheeks. She looked away and pulled off the rain jacket.

If she kept eye contact, she'd start grinning and stammering along with blushing.

"I was out walking the beach. From the looks of things, everyone here made you comfortable while you waited."

The interns all grinned and hurried to talk over one another about how they'd completed their morning fieldwork. Danielle lifted her hands. "You're fine. I'm not that much of an evil boss that I'm going to get angry about you being excited when a famous basketball player comes into the office."

"You have softened up," Jacobe said. "The Danielle I knew was always on task and never took a break."

She lifted her chin and met his eye. "That was the Danielle I allowed you to know."

"I think I got a glimpse of the more laid-back Danielle once." The corner of his mouth lifted in a smile full of the sinful secrets of that more laid-back Danielle.

She ignored the butterflies crashing around her stomach like drunken seagulls. "You said you wanted to see me—well, I'm here. Let's go to my office." She looked at everyone in the room. "You all can get back to work."

Jacobe grinned and strolled over to her. "That's the Danielle I know and love."

She snorted. "Love had nothing to do with our relationship." She spun away and marched from the kitchen. One of the interns winked at her as Danielle passed. She could only imagine the thoughts going through her mind.

She made her way down the hall to the last door on the right. Jacobe's footsteps followed.

"You're wrong," Jacobe said. "There were a lot of things I loved about you."

"What, my badgering you to come to our study sessions on time, or my endless lectures about what you could be contributing to make the world a better place?"

She stepped over the threshold into her office, but a tug on the back of her sweater kept her from taking another step. She faltered, then quickly turned. Jacobe let go.

"These little sweaters you wear. I loved those."

Danielle looked down at her rather unremarkable outfit: gray slacks, a black-and-yellow polka-dot blouse and a bright yellow cardigan, then back up at him. "My cardigans?"

"Yes, you're just as sexy in those now as you were then." He lifted a hand and reached for her face. Danielle jerked back before he touched her. He grinned. "I was only going to compliment you on the glasses. I like these better than the ones you used to wear." When he reached forward this time, she didn't pull away. Jacobe ran a finger over the hinges and lightly brushed her face. "Between the glasses and the sweaters you've got the sexy, good-girl vibe going on. I always knew there was passion in you for more than just class work."

Her body went up in flames. Taking a step back, Danielle inhaled a deep, shaky breath. "If you're here to repeat your request from Saturday night, then you've wasted your time."

She wished her office was big enough to stalk to the other side and put a decent enough space between them. Instead, there was little extra space in the small room. Between her desk, file cabinets and plastic tubs filled with materials they used for various functions, she barely had a clear path from the door to her seat behind the desk.

Jacobe followed her farther into the office. His huge, muscled form soaked up all the remaining space in the room. He pushed the door closed. When he faced her again, thankfully, he didn't step closer and leaned against the door, instead.

"That's not why I'm here. One of the reasons I came by is to apologize for the other night."

She'd opened her mouth in preparation for a rebuff. She snapped it closed. "Come again? You're apologizing?"

"Don't sound so surprised. I am capable of admitting when I'm wrong. You remember that much about me."

She did, actually. He may have given her a hard time when she fussed about him keeping her waiting and always had a reason for why he was late, but he never tried to blame his inability to keep to their schedule on anyone but himself. She would have had a much easier time not lusting after him if he'd blamed others for his problems.

"I do."

"I am sorry about approaching you like that. I had a bad game, as you saw. When I spotted you, nothing but good memories of that night popped up. I can't lie. I wanted you again."

Her knees went weak. She sat on the edge of her desk to hide the effect. "Oh. Well, good memories or not, I wasn't there to relive that one night."

"I guessed as much when you stalked out mad as hell. I still want you, but I'm willing to earn my way into your bed. Not assume you'll automatically let me there."

Awareness—no, anticipation buzzed through her body. "You're here to let me know you're planning to seduce me?"

He straightened from the door and shook his head. "I do think you should know that I'm perfectly willing to pick up where we left off, but that's not why I'm here.

The other reason for this visit is because I need a favor that involves the River Watchers."

Her brain fought to keep up. He wanted a repeat of that night? That shouldn't make her so giddy. Pushing the giddiness firmly aside, she focused on the second statement. "A favor? Really?"

"Really."

"What kind of favor?"

He rubbed his hands together and examined the various framed awards and news clippings on her office wall. "I'd like to volunteer, do some things to improve my image by helping the environment." He focused back on her.

"Why?" She crossed her arms and studied him.

"Out of the goodness of my heart."

She shook her head. "Not buying it. Try again."

He grinned, completely unperturbed by her reply. "You're still a hard-ass."

"I still know when you're avoiding getting to the point. Why do you suddenly want to help an organization you hadn't heard of before Saturday?"

"I've got a five-game suspension. It's going to be announced later today. I need something to boost my image in my free time." He said "free time" as if it were a bad word. For him, she guessed it was. She could imagine how frustrated she'd be if someone took her work away from her.

"What do you have in mind?"

"I checked your website and saw that you have a few things coming up. A cleanup and silent auction. I'll come help, invite the media, and show everyone that I'm more than just a distraction for the team."

"You've got it all figured out."

"Those were just my thoughts. You're the head of

this thing. You tell me where you need me to be and I'll be there."

She frowned, not sure if she liked the idea. The part of her that needed ticket sales for the gala knew having the star of the Gators attend her events would bring much needed attention, ticket sales and donations the River Watchers desperately needed.

The skeptical part thought this was an offer too good to be true. In her memory, those types of situations always ended with her left behind and forgotten.

"I can tell you're not convinced," he said. "I know having me around might cause a headache for you guys. I don't want to cause you too much trouble. If you'd like, we can go out to dinner and discuss the arrangements."

Skeptical, Danielle smirked. "We don't need to go to dinner to discuss you volunteering here."

"I know that. The dinner is my way of getting you out on a date." He held up two fingers. "Two birds with one stone."

Danielle stood and placed her hands on her hips. "Volunteering isn't how you earn your way into my bed."

Jacobe stepped away from the door. With one long stride, he stood before her in the pitifully small office. "Volunteering is only about my basketball image. I came here straight from a meeting with my agent, coach, PR and one of the owners. My suspension right before play-offs is making them question resigning me next year."

Danielle doubted the Gators would turn away a talent like Jacobe just because of one disciplinary action. But he had been traded because of his outbursts. His point might be valid, but the look in his eyes said something else was on the line.

"What's really at stake? This isn't just about re-signing with the Gators."

His head tilted to the side and surprise filled his gaze. "Why do you think it's something else?"

"Just a feeling."

He was quiet for a few seconds before speaking up. "Are you in the habit of turning down people who want to volunteer?"

Fine. He could keep his secrets. As long as he understood she wasn't going to fall at his feet just because he was bringing publicity to the River Watchers.

"We can discuss volunteer opportunities right here in the office. It doesn't have to be over dinner."

"If it'll make you feel better, we can do that. I still want to take you out tonight." He tugged on the edge of her sweater, right above her breasts. "Consider a date as the second half of my apology."

"The first half was more than enough."

"Then consider it two old friends catching up."

"We were hardly friends."

"Then accept the fact that I just want to spend a little time with you. No expectations and no strings attached." He took her hand in his and threaded their fingers together. "Believe it or not, I've thought of you a few times over the years and my thoughts weren't always about that night. I really do want to go out with you tonight."

His eyes never left hers. There was nothing sly or mocking in his gaze. The look, his smile and the delicious heat from his body delivered a sensual knockout that nearly stole her voice.

"Jacobe, we shouldn't blur the lines."

"Danielle, even if I found another organization to volunteer for I'd still be here asking you out." He pulled slightly on her hand until she shifted closer to him. "One date. That's all. Okay?"

His thumb brushed lazily across the inside of her palm. The light touch sent delicious shivers over her body. His gaze grabbed hers and held it hostage. Danielle was lost in the brown depths and lulled by the slow play of his hands on her. Jacobe's gaze lowered to her lips. Danielle felt every excited beat of her heart throughout her body.

She nodded. "One date."

His eyes heated to delicious pools of melted chocolate. He leaned closer. He was going to kiss her. Danielle's heart jackhammered.

She jumped back. He immediately let go. Her arm hit a small stack of papers on her desk. The sheets flew to the floor. Turning away from him, she quickly bent to pick them up. "Um…as for volunteering, I'll let you talk with Debra. She helps coordinate volunteers." She slapped the papers on her desk. He stood in the middle of the small path to the door. She tried to quickly scoot past him without touching.

Her breasts brushed his chest. White-hot desire slammed into her. Her nipples tightened. Danielle jerked forward and almost tripped. When he reached out to help her, she held her hand away and righted herself.

"No worries, I'm good." She glanced at his face. He was watching her, smiling. Danielle looked away and opened the door. "I'll get Debra." She hurried out of the room before she turned into even more of a stuttering ninny.

Chapter 4

"What's really going on between you and Jacobe?" Debra asked as she and Danielle skimmed a row of party dresses in Revelry Dress Shop.

The second she'd agreed to a date with Jacobe, Danielle realized she had nothing to wear for a date with a NBA superstar. Her dating life of the past few years had been filled with other men from the conservation field. Hiking, biking, and kayaking with the occasional dinner at Applebees. Jacobe hadn't said where he was taking her, only that he'd text with the details.

"Nothing. It's just two friends catching up." She picked up a pink sequined scrap of material she assumed was supposed to be a dress. "What's this? Why did you bring me here? I said I needed help picking an outfit for a date, not prom."

Debra laughed and pushed back several other dresses on the rack in front of her. "You said you didn't have anything to wear."

"I thought we'd just go to the mall."

Debra leaned close. "You're going out with Jacobe Jenkins." Her voice was low as if conveying a big secret. "He'll probably take you to a nightclub. Do you have a nightclub dress?"

"No." She eyed Debra's Supernatural T-shirt and gray earrings in the shape of a skeletal hand. "Do you?"

"No, but if I needed one this is where I'd go. Now look." Debra pointed to the dresses.

Danielle sighed and looked through the dresses. "This isn't necessary. I just needed a simple dress and a new sweater. This isn't going to be a big deal."

"You don't know that. He came all the way downtown to apologize for whatever he did to piss you off after the game."

Danielle hadn't told Debra exactly what Jacobe said. Doing so would require revealing they'd slept together in college. She'd just said he'd been the same jerk she remembered.

"He's volunteering to help us," Debra said.

"To help his image."

"But it still helps us. And he asked you out. For once don't be so doubtful and just have a little fun."

"I'm not being doubtful, I'm being realistic. In what world does the professional basketball star fall for the conservation girl?"

"I don't know. Yours maybe."

"Look, I've been here before. Professional athletes have an unlimited access to money and women. Long term relationships aren't on their agenda."

"Hold up. Wait a minute." Debra turned to face Danielle and leaned one arm on top of the dress rack. "You've been here? I need the, who, what, when and where?"

Danielle nearly swore. She didn't like talking about what happened with her ex-boyfriend. She'd never mentioned him to Debra. She straightened her glasses and turned back to the dresses. "It's a figure of speech."

"Spill it, Danielle. Come on, I thought we were friends."

"We are."

"Then tell me the story. You hear all of my baggage. Spill yours."

Danielle stopped searching to glance at Debra. She had the determined look that said she wasn't going to let the subject die. Why not tell her? Maybe then she'd realize this *date* with Jacobe meant nothing.

"I dated Luke Kinard in college," Danielle kind of mumbled.

Debra's jaw dropped. "Luke Kinard? Like, professional football player, Luke Kinard?"

Danielle tried to give a no-big-deal shrug. This is why she didn't talk about Luke much. People got overly excited about a disappointing time in her life. "Yeah. We met at an Earth Day clean up my sophomore year and hit it off. We dated through college. I knew he wanted to go pro, but we both never really thought he would. He wasn't drafted, but he decided to try to be a walk on in Philadelphia. He said if he made it, we'd move to Philly and get married."

A line of confusion formed between Debra's brows. "He made it. He's one of their biggest defensive linemen."

"After he go the offer, he told me about the women who throw themselves at rookies. How much time he'll have to spend at practices and learning the play book. He didn't break up with me. I don't think he wanted to, but I could tell he didn't want to miss out on all the *perks* of being in the league. So, I broke up with him. Took the job with the River Watchers and moved on."

"That sucks."

"No, it's reality."

"But weren't you upset?"

She had been upset. Hurt. She and Luke had talked about marriage. They both had similar interests. She'd loved him, and she believed he had loved her. He would have tried to make their relationship work. She hadn't wanted them to end up hating each other because of the pressures from being in the league.

"It was better that way. We're still friends. I meet up with him for lunch whenever he's in town."

"Wait? The friend Luke you meet up with every so often is Luke Kinard? Geez, Danielle, I can't believe you didn't tell me Luke was *Luke Kinard!*" Debra sounded a little hurt by the revelation.

"Only because I didn't want to sound like I was bragging. We're just friends now."

"Friends or not, that's important background information. Dang, first you know Jacobe Jenkins now you're Luke Kinard's ex-girlfriend. What next, is Halle Berry your cousin?"

Danielle laughed. "No. There are no other celebrities in my background."

Danielle's phone chimed with the text message alert. She pulled the phone from her purse. "It's from Jacobe." She read the message. "He wants to go bowling. He's asking if I mind."

"Bowling?"

Danielle grinned. "Yes! Thank goodness." She put the pink monstrosity back on the rack. "I really didn't want to wear a sequined party dress and go to a nightclub." She texted back that bowling was cool. "Let's get out of here."

"Bowling?" Debra said again and followed Danielle to the door. "That's not very romantic."

"Exactly. What did I tell you? We're just two friends catching up with each other. There's nothing that's going to come of this."

"I swore there were sparks between you two."

Sparks, flames, knee melting electric energy. All of that flowed through Danielle whenever Jacobe was near. She'd been burned by that flame before. She wasn't about to get burned again.

Danielle pushed open the door of the dress shop and marched out to the warm spring air. "Forget sparks. All I want, and need, from Jacobe is his help selling tickets to the gala to save the River Watchers."

Jacobe chose bowling for several reasons. One, he liked to bowl. He'd bought the bowling alley after the owner wanted to let it go a year ago. He frequented the place enough to not be mobbed by fans. Guaranteeing a little bit of privacy for him and Danielle without being too intimate. He also remembered seeing Danielle at the bowling alley in college a few times and hoped she still enjoyed playing.

"I hope you don't mind bowling?" he asked as he opened one of the double glass doors to let her in. In his other hand he carried the bag that held his bowling ball and shoes.

The sounds of music along with the crack of bowling balls against pins filled the air. She wore a pair of sexy black jeans that hugged her hips, a ruffled white top and a cute black cardigan with a flower on the breast. She wasn't wearing heels and he could look down at the top of her head, making him infinitely aware of how small and feminine she was.

"I don't mind," she said. "I haven't bowled in a while. This might be fun. Don't you own this place?"

The smell of her light flowery perfume drifted around him as she passed. He took a deep breath to take in more of her. "You know I own this place?"

"You're a local celebrity. I saw something on a news report once."

"I sponsor most of the leagues that play here. When the previous owner started to shut it down, I stepped in so they wouldn't have to find a new place to play or quit all together."

She glanced up at him as they made their way to get bowling shoes. "Wow, that's a lot of investment."

"I like bowling."

"I do, too, but not enough to buy a bowling alley. Why do you love bowling so much?" Her big brown eyes were filled with curiosity.

"I said I like bowling. Not that I love it," he deflected.

"To buy this place so the teams could keep playing says you love it. Why?"

He shrugged. "Just do. I played a lot as a kid." He turned away from her curious gaze to look at the guy behind the shoe-exchange counter. "What's up, Dennis. I brought a friend in for a few rounds."

Danielle turned around to greet Dennis. Usually, when asked why he'd bought a bowling alley, he answered because he liked bowling. At that response, people just moved on. He didn't get into why he liked bowling. After his dad was killed, his grandfather would take Jacobe bowling on Wednesday nights. They'd kept up the routine for years until his grandfather passed away. Those Wednesday night bowling sessions had kept Jacobe sane after the craziness of his dad's passing. But to tell Danielle that meant he had to reveal too much of himself.

"I hope you have a good arm," Dennis was saying to Danielle. He pointed to Jacobe. "This guy is serious about bowling."

Danielle handed over her flats and took the shoes Dennis held out to her. "I'm decent. I think I can hold my own against him."

"I wish you luck then." Dennis looked at Jacobe. "You got your shoes, or you need a pair?"

Jacobe held up the shoes in his hand. "Brought mine."

"You have your own shoes?" Danielle said as they walked toward the first alley. It was against the far wall, with two empty alleys between them and the other people out bowling. Jacobe smiled and nodded at the regulars he recognized.

"Yeah."

"But you just *like* bowling. I think there's more to the story."

She smiled at him, and it was so cute he couldn't help but smile back. "Maybe there is, but I'm not ready to tell the story." Her brows drew together and he knew she was about to go digging again. He leaned down and lowered his voice. "We've got to save something for pillow talk."

She waved a hand as if his words were ridiculous, but he caught the spark of interest that had briefly lit up her eyes. "Stop that. I thought we were just here as old friends."

"You said we were hardly friends."

"I had to say that. I wasn't sure if you meant what you said about volunteering or not. But after listening to you and Debra set up your volunteer schedule, I figured you are serious."

"Very serious. I need some good press."

"Because of the suspension?" She walked away to check out the balls on the rack near their alley.

"That and I've got plans. I don't need people thinking that all I am is a bad temper and partying." Jacobe sat behind the controls to set up the automatic scoring for the game.

Danielle came over and sat next to him. "What type of plans? Hey, I bowl first."

"Excuse me," he teased. He deleted his name and put in hers first.

"So, what are your plans?"

"To be considered one of the best players in the league."

Danielle turned in her seat to face him. "That's a wish, not a plan."

"What do you mean?"

"I want to be considered a leader in my field, but just because I want that doesn't mean it'll happen. Not without a plan with real goals to get there."

"Okay, Professor Stewart, what are your goals?"

"First is showing genuine enthusiasm for what I do. I want to make a difference. Not just here but on a larger scale. I pick projects that will have a measurable impact when they're done, like shutting down Clear Water."

"Clear Water?" Jacobe leaned down to pull off his shoes and slip on his bowling shoes.

Danielle's brows rose to her hairline, and her eyes were wide. "Do you live under a rock?"

He shrugged. "Apparently so. Tell me what it is."

"They're a sewer provider who can't properly treat the sewage coming to their plant. They dumped tons of bacteria-laden water into the creeks for years. I fought to get their permit enforced. Major fines were levied and they have to put together a corrective plan to either tie into a better system or shut down."

"Wow. You did that?" He was impressed.

She leaned back and straightened her glasses. She looked embarrassed by his praise. "Well, not just me."

"They're shutting down?"

"They're trying to expand. They want to dump into Springfield Creek!"

She looked at him like he should be outraged. He shook his head. "You need to school me again, Professor."

She did. For the next few rounds of bowling, she updated him on her efforts to prevent Clear Water from expanding and dumping into the creek. Jacobe was amazed that all of this was happening right here, and that more people weren't talking about it.

She obviously was an advocate for her work. Her passion to make things right in the world hadn't changed. What, or who, else was she passionate about? He'd experienced the heat of her fire during their one night together. He didn't for a moment think she was seeing someone else. Danielle wasn't the type to hang out with him if she had a man, but there had to be something else that excited her. If not, he'd be more than willing to bring fun into her life.

"You know," Jacobe said, after he'd bowled a spare and was coming back to where Danielle was picking up her ball to bowl. "Back in college I knew you were into this stuff, but I thought—I don't know—that you were just being a Goody Two-shoes."

Her laugh was incredulous. "What?"

"I mean, I didn't realize that you really cared about

this. Not just because it seemed like the right thing to do or that everyone else was doing it. You're kind of impressive."

She fiddled with her glasses again and glanced away. "I'm not impressive. I'm just a hard worker. You're the one people think of as being impressive. Famous basketball star and all that. People listen when you talk just because you're a celebrity." She met his gaze. "I know you don't want to tell me your ultimate plan and that you're only volunteering to help your image, but thank you anyway. You'll get us the attention we need. That'll go a long way to help me."

She walked to the head of the aisle to bowl. Jacobe sat in the plastic chair behind the controls to watch her. Danielle was far more impressive than he. He wanted the recognition for being the best; she wanted to make sure people had clean water. He cared about boys who didn't know what direction to take. After his spiral when his dad died, and later discovering he wasn't the father of Christy's son, he recognized the need for more male mentors out there. He funded programs for that, but he wasn't as driven to that cause as Danielle was to hers. He'd had nothing but basketball and anger. If he lost basketball, did he really just want to be left with anger?

Danielle rolled a strike and jumped up and down. Jacobe clapped and smiled at her. That was the first strike she'd bowled all night. The bounce of her luscious breasts while she jumped distracted him. His clapping slowed.

A quick vision of her on top of the dresser in a long-ago college room, her dress pulled down and her soft breasts in his hands while his mouth kissed and sucked on nipples as sweet as candy flashed through his mind.

That night had been too fast, too rushed and hurried. Next time he'd be sure to take his time and kiss every inch of her body.

Jacobe looked away and forced the memory out of his head. His brain cleared, but his body didn't follow suit. His blood heated and his dick swelled just enough to let him know that if he didn't control his thoughts he'd have a full on erection in no time. He didn't want her tonight.

Yes, you do.

Okay, he wouldn't turn her down tonight, but that wasn't the point of this date. He'd tasted Danielle, then walked away without a backward glance after Christy tricked him. He wouldn't let her think that he cared only about sex when it came to her.

What the hell, Jacobe? You want a relationship, now? No, that answer was clear. Women like Danielle wanted commitments. He no longer did commitments.

"Hey, you okay?" Danielle said.

Jacobe had lowered his head, his eyes closed as first the memory, then the scary thought of a relationship entered his mind. He opened his eyes and slowly lifted his head. He tried to give her a smile but feared it looked as force as he felt.

"Yeah, I'm good."

Her answering smile was open and excited, so he assumed his didn't look as bad as he thought. "Did you see my strike?"

"I did. Still not enough to catch up with me." He pointed to the score.

Danielle rolled her eyes and hit him on the shoulder. "We're only halfway through the game. And this ain't the basketball court. I'm only a few points behind. Game time, baby."

True. If she hit a few more, they'd be neck and neck.

Jacobe had stood and picked up his ball when a thought struck him. He turned back to Danielle. "Do you hate me?"

"What?"

"Do you hate me for not calling you?"

Her smile slowly melted away. Her shoulders straightened and she sat up in the seat. When she met his gaze her eyes were serious. "I don't know what I expected after that night. Everything happened so quickly. I came to show you I wasn't afraid of the spark between us. Next thing I know we're…you know. It was great, but I didn't think anything too serious would happen afterward. Certainly no expectations for a relationship."

She sounded so calm. So over it. How could it not have bothered her when it had bothered him occasionally over the years?

He took a step toward her. "If I would have called and asked you to date me, would you have considered it?"

She shrugged and looked at the control board. "I don't know."

He had a feeling she was lying. "I'm sorry I never called."

"Don't be. I moved on. I wasn't sitting around campus pining for you."

"I didn't think you were."

She nodded. "Good."

"Did you start seeing someone else?" Why in the world was he torturing himself with that question?

Her gaze met his. "I did."

He tried to remember if there'd been a particular guy sniffing around her that year, but came up a blank. "Who?"

She raised a brow. "Does it really matter?"

No, it didn't, not really. He didn't want to know her past any more than he wanted her digging into his. "You're right."

"Besides, I saw you with Christy afterward and assumed you two were together."

His shoulders stiffened and he gripped the ball in his hands. "We weren't that night. I wouldn't have had sex with you if I'd still been with her."

The rigid set to Danielle's posture relaxed and she nodded. "I know."

That surprised him. "I wouldn't have believed you thought so highly of me."

"I did. I was around you enough to know how many women tried to sleep with you, and how you turned each of them down. It was an admirable trait."

"Just one admirable trait. Are you sure there weren't others?"

"You had a few, but that's the one that really struck me as odd. As popular as you were, and as conceited as you were." He opened his mouth to argue and she held up a finger. "Don't interrupt, you were."

Jacobe closed his mouth and motioned with his hand for her to continue. Who was he kidding? He had enough confidence in his game to be considered conceited.

"I expected you to take up every willing female that came your way. Especially since it seemed like every other day you and Christy were arguing."

That was true. People used to ask him why he stayed with Christy. He'd never felt the need to say anything other than she had his back. He never talked about how his dad's death was proof cheating wasn't worth it, or that Christy had been the girl he'd fallen in love with in the middle of his grief. Right before he really became good at ball and women who'd once ignored him were suddenly offering him sex left and right. Danielle deserved more than that simple explanation.

"Christy looked out for me back in high school before I'd really blown up. I was a good player, but after my dad died, I started skipping school, being a smartass in class and playing pranks just to frustrate the teachers. One day one of my pranks went too far."

"What did you do?"

"Stupid, really. My English teacher gave an assignment. Write a paper on the great contributors of American literature. I didn't like anything we read that year, so my paper was on why English literature was better."

"That wasn't the topic."

"I know. Anyway, he threatened to fail me. I got mad because if I failed I couldn't play ball. I put some fireworks in his desk and set them off right before class. There was smoke and the fire department was called."

Danielle's hand was over her mouth as she laughed. "No."

He nodded. "Yeah. It was bad. I would have been suspended, maybe expelled." His laughter died. "Christy said she did it. Took the suspension and everything. When I asked why, she said because she knew I needed another chance before I screwed up my future. I did. After my dad died, I hid the hurt behind smiles, jokes and basketball. Everyone viewed me as this star player or this screw up in class. Christy was the first person to call me on my crap. If she hadn't said that, I would have ruined my chances. That was the year I really got on the radar of college recruiters. If I'd been expelled, that wouldn't have happened."

Dozens of questions swam in her chocolate eyes. He'd revealed too much about himself in that story.

Stuff that he didn't want others to know. He hadn't even told Christy why he'd stayed with her for so long.

"Why did you come to the party that night?" he asked, before she could start a line of questions he didn't want to answer.

She shrugged and looked away, but tugged on the front of her sweater. "You made it seem like I didn't know how to party. That annoyed me. I came to show you I could have fun."

"You came in a dress that made me want nothing more than to see you out of it. It was a pleasant surprise."

The memory of that night flooded his mind. Danielle in a sleeveless black dress that hugged every one of her curves. *"You wore that dress for me?"*

"I wore this dress for myself."

"Will you take it off for me later?"

Damn that line had been cocky, and corny. She'd rolled her eyes before grinning and walking away. He'd followed her like a dope for the rest of the night.

His eyes met hers. The tip of her tongue ran across her full bottom lip. Her breasts rose as she took a deep breath. He licked his own lips and remembered the sweet taste of her.

"Are you sure you didn't wear that dress for me?"

Danielle stood abruptly. "Want some nachos?"

He wanted to say no and continue their conversation, but he didn't want to push. "Sure. Get a pizza, too. Or whatever you want to eat. Tell them you're with me. It'll be on the house."

She nodded then turned toward the concession. Jacobe turned to bowl.

"Jacobe," she called. He turned to face her. Her full lips were raised in a teasing grin. "I guess you learned

I could handle you after all." She spun away and hurried to the concession.

Jacobe grinned and turned back to bowl. Danielle Stewart was full of surprises.

He didn't like talking about himself. Danielle realized that about halfway through their date. Most people would respect that he didn't share much and move on. Most people hadn't known him in college and remembered that he'd been cocky and fun loving, but also open and straightforward. Now he was closed off. Still charming, but guarded. The need to get to the bottom of a situation was one of her strongest traits and biggest flaws. Trying to unravel the secrets of a guy like Jacobe could result in her becoming too involved with a man who'd proved he could easily walk away from her.

"I had fun tonight," Danielle said as they walked to his car. She hadn't known what to expect before going out with him. She had known she would need to limit the opportunities for him to suck her into his web of temptation as he'd done earlier that day in her office. Bowling had been perfect. Minimal chances to touch or get lost staring into his eyes.

"Then I'll have to take you bowling again."

She turned to walk backward and face him. "I offered one date. No expectations and no strings attached."

Jacobe took her hand in his and pulled her closer. She was so startled by the movement that she didn't pull back. "What do I have to do to get you to go out with me again?"

He was so tempting. She'd get wrapped up in Jacobe and lose her heart. It had been easier in college when he'd left because they hadn't been together long enough for her to fall in love with him. That didn't mean she didn't know how much it hurt to have someone she loved leave her behind. She wasn't going through that again.

"I don't view first dates as an interview for marriage, but it is a chance for me to decide if I want another date and possibly a serious relationship. I'm looking for a commitment one day. What are you looking for?"

She would not normally be so candid on a first date, but she had to with Jacobe. He might be more guarded, but his flirtatious side hadn't gone anywhere. She could only imagine the number of women he went out with. He needed to realize she wasn't interested in being his short-term bedroom playmate.

Jacobe stopped and let go of her hand. "I'm not looking for anything serious right now."

She wasn't surprised, but that didn't stop the small tickle of disappointment in her chest. "That's cool. I just need you to understand what I'm looking for. If you're not interested in the same, fine. I'm happy to work with you at the River Watchers, but that has to be it. If my position means you'd rather work for another organization I understand."

His brows drew together. "I told you helping the River Watchers is about my image, not a sneaky way to get you in bed. Volunteering will show critics I'm not spending my five-game suspension sitting around sulking or starting fights like everyone expects me to."

The need to know more perked up. "Why do you start fights? In college you were always the life of the party, not a fighter."

"When you're really pissed off, it's easy to take your anger out on other people."

"About your son?"

His body tensed. "He's not my son." Jacobe spit out the words in a hard and tight tone.

Danielle flinched and crossed her arms over her chest. Her cheeks burned with embarrassment. She never should have brought that up.

Jacobe stepped closer and used his finger to lift her chin. "I'm sorry. I don't like talking about that situation."

"I won't bring it up again."

He nodded and dropped his hand. "Right now my goal is to convince people in the league that I'm not the hothead I used to be. I went through some stuff and it overshadowed my game. I can't let that happen anymore. I've got plans. This suspension could hurt those plans."

"Plans with the Gators?"

"I'm happy to play for the Gators. What we've done is phenomenal, but if I get the chance to play for an even better team I won't turn it down. I'll do whatever I can to take my career to the next level. If the Gators don't believe in me anymore, I don't need other teams to be afraid to sign me. You can understand that much."

She could. As a Gators fan, she didn't want him to leave. He was an asset to the team—no one could deny that. As someone who yearned to find someplace where she felt like she belonged, she could understand his ambition to leave. She'd loved her work with the River Watchers until Liberty got on the board and began threatening her job. Not having the full backing of your organization left you feeling lost.

She turned and walked toward his car. Jacobe fell into step beside her, following her to the passenger side. Instead of opening the door, he leaned a hand against the roof and turned to her.

"As for what you said earlier, about wanting a relationship. I hear you." He reached out to fiddle with the chiffon petals of the flower on her cardigan. "I brought you bowling because I want to get to know Danielle, the woman, instead of just going off the memories of the Danielle who tutored me in biology."

"You can get to know me as a friend and colleague."

The corner of his mouth lifted. He stared at his fingers on the flower at her chest. "I'm always open to a friends-with-benefits arrangement."

He met her eye, slid a few inches closer. For a spit second she was tempted to say yes. Reality and common sense prevailed. "I'm not good at separating sex and feelings."

His body instantly stilled and his lips pressed into a faint frown. He dropped his hand from her flower and leaned back. "That night, were you…"

She shook her head. "No. I meant what I said about not being mad about the outcome, but our night together did teach me that I'm not good at the love 'em and leave 'em philosophy when it comes to relationships. I'm also not good at having one-night stands."

His retreat bolstered her confidence. She needed to see this. Needed to be reminded that Jacobe was looking for fun and nothing more. Better to be disappointed now than heartbroken later.

Danielle reached for the door handle. "It's getting late."

He stepped back and opened the door. "You're right. I should get you home."

Jacobe didn't say much on the drive to her place. She was dying to know what was going through his head. Was he angry that he'd wasted a date with a woman he wouldn't easily get into bed? Did he even care enough to be disappointed? An online search quickly revealed he had no shortage of women interested in him and that he was rarely photographed twice with the same woman. Her rejection might be just a minimal blip on his radar when it came to women.

When they arrived at her place, a small ranch-style home that she'd purchased the year before, he came around and opened the door for her. His hand was warm and solid when he placed it on her lower back to walk her to her front door. The porch light flickered, casting the porch in shadows. She'd been meaning to change that bulb.

"Thanks again," she said, getting her keys out of her purse.

Jacobe took her elbow in his hand and turned her to face him. He stood so close that she had to tilt her head back even farther to meet his gaze. In the unsteady light of the porch, she couldn't make out the expression in his eyes.

"I respect your honesty, Danielle." His other hand came up to brush across her chin. "Don't think this kiss means otherwise."

Her heart fluttered and anticipation tingled every inch of skin on her body. "Who said you could kiss me?"

His dark eyes met hers and the corner of his mouth tilted up in a smile that would make a nun drop her panties. "Tell me I can't and I won't."

The air crackled around them. Sparks of heat filled her chest. Her eyes lowered to his lips. Full and soft. Based on the smoldering heat in his eyes, desperately wanting to touch hers. A kiss wasn't sex. It was just a kiss.

"One kiss," she whispered.

"Good."

His lips brushed hers before he slowly pulled her lower lip between his. The kiss was a slow tasting. Not one long press of the lips, but several small sexy touches and pulls of his mouth on hers. With each sweep her body heated and tightened with need. Danielle shifted forward, closing the distance between them. Finally, his tongue slipped across her lower lip. Desire pulsed through her midsection. Jacobe's strong arm slipped around her waist and drew her flush against the hardness of his body.

He was so much taller. She automatically went onto her toes, parting her lips so he could deepen the kiss. The arm around her waist tightened, and a second later Jacobe lifted her off her feet. Her breasts pressed into the firmness of his chest, her arms wrapped around his neck. She shifted and her body rubbed against the growing bulk of his erection. Memories of the full length of him filling her completely flooded her mind. Heat pooled low in her midsection and between her legs.

Jacobe sucked in a breath and broke the kiss. His breathing was just as harsh and heavy as hers in the quiet darkness of her porch. She could feel him pulsing, growing between them. She bit her lower lip to keep from moaning and begging for more.

He slowly lowered her back to her feet and took one determined step backward. He cupped her chin and ran his thumb over her sensitive lower lip. "One kiss," he said. "I keep my word." He leaned down and pressed another quick kiss to her lips. When he pulled back, she couldn't stop herself from leaning forward to prolong the touch.

"Good night, Danielle."

Jacobe turned, jumped the three steps from her porch to the ground and strode purposefully back to his car.

Danielle stood on her porch and watched him drive away until the taillights disappeared.

She pressed a hand to her pounding heart. "Don't ever kiss him again if you want to keep your sanity," she whispered.

Chapter 5

"How are you handling the suspension?" Isaiah asked Jacobe.

He, Kevin and Will, were all seated outside next to the full court in the backyard of Jacobe's riverfront home. Jacobe's suspension prevented him from going to the stadium, attending practices and doing anything related to the team. He'd expected to be completely ignored by his teammates. To his surprise, Kevin, Will and Isaiah had shown up on their off day to give him an update on what had happened at practice and the plans for their next game.

"I'm going to volunteer with the River Watchers." He palmed the basketball in his hands. They'd played one game shortly after the guys had arrived. Jacobe and Isaiah had won against Kevin and Will. "And beat Kevin in pickup games."

Kevin smirked "I'm just trying to make you feel better."

Isaiah laughed. "If that's what you've got to tell your-self."

Kevin laughed along with Will before he looked back at Jacobe. "Why the River Watchers?"

"I'm going to volunteer with them. Do some good stuff for the environment, try to show I'm more than a troublemaker."

Will frowned and ran a hand over the full beard covering the lower half of his face. "Don't you think you'd get more brownie points showing up at the place that you give money to for mentoring?"

Jacobe shrugged. "Maybe, but what can I say to a group of boys? Hold on to your tempers and act like gentlemen? I can't even do that myself. This will give me a new angle, and it's a local thing. If I can get the locals to care, then the management will, too."

"River Watchers," Isaiah said suspiciously. "Isn't that the group the woman you tried to hook up with the other night works for?"

"Yeah."

Kevin nodded his head and gave Jacobe a sly look. "Now I get it. You're trying to get in good with her because she turned you down."

"Nah, it's not like that."

Will's eyes turned skeptical. "You're not trying to hook up with her?"

Jacobe thought about the kiss and how he'd had to call on every ounce of gentlemanly behavior he'd ever picked up not to press to get inside Danielle's house and in her bed. Danielle wanted a commitment. He didn't do commitments. He wasn't opening himself up to a woman like that again.

"That's not why I'm volunteering. She'd see through that, anyway," he said. "Me and her knew each other back in college. I wouldn't mind hooking up with her, but she made it very clear she's looking for forever. I stepped back."

Isaiah stood and held up his hands for Jacobe to toss him the ball. "Figures."

Jacobe threw him the ball, then frowned. "What's that supposed to mean?"

"You aren't ready to settle down. Figures you'd step back," Isaiah said, dribbling the ball.

Will sat forward. "But you're still going to work with her?"

"Why not? Her organization does good things—we can help each other out."

Kevin shook his head. "It's never a good idea to work with a woman you want to sleep with. That never turns out well for me."

Isaiah laughed and passed the ball to Kevin. "That's because you don't know how to say no to a beautiful woman."

Kevin stood, dribbled and threw the ball back. "Why should I?"

Jacobe shifted in his seat so he could better watch Kevin and Isaiah. "Just because it never worked for you doesn't mean it won't for me. I can handle working with Danielle."

Kevin raised a brow. "And if she just happens to forget she's looking for a commitment and you two end up in bed together? What then?"

"He's right, man," Will said. "It's never a good idea to mix business and pleasure, especially for a guy like you."

"A guy like me?"

"Yeah, you." Isaiah dribbled the ball between his legs, then jumped to shoot for the basket. It went through with a swoosh. "You're so anti-relationship and up-front about not wanting to settle down that women try even harder to change your mind. She'll end up falling in love with you."

Jacobe laughed. "Doubtful. I don't think I'm the type of guy she'd want to be with long-term."

He was relieved she hadn't hated him all these years, but what had she meant when she said their time had taught her she wasn't into one-night stands anymore? Had she had others? The thought made him tense with jealousy. She'd mentioned moving on after he left. If she hadn't done the one-night stands, was there a serious boyfriend in her past? More than one serious relationship? If so, what had happened with those guys?

Isaiah had run to get the ball and jogged back over to them. "You make women fall in love with you without even trying. Believe me, she's going to fall. You always have the ones who want forever coming on to you. Me, I always end up with the crazy women who aren't about anything."

Kevin snorted and slapped the ball out of Isaiah's hand. "That's because you're trying too hard to find this perfect woman to marry. I'm telling you, she ain't out there."

"I want kids one day."

"You don't need a wife to have kids," Kevin said. "Take one of mine."

They all laughed. Kevin had four kids, two with his ex-wife and two from a woman he'd dated after his divorce. He took care of them all but had made it clear he didn't want more, going so far as to get a vasectomy in the off-season.

"I'd rather have my own kids than bum one of yours."

Jacobe held up his hands. "Can we stop talking about

kids? You're making my nuts uncomfortable. I'm not trying to make Danielle fall in love with me, marry me, or have any kids. I'm not looking for that at all."

Isaiah studied him closely. "I think you'll change your mind one day."

Jacobe shook his head. "Hell no, I'm not changing my mind. I'm not setting myself up to get played for a fool again, and you know just as well as I do how hard it is to find a woman who's for real in this business. I'm only worrying about making the suits happy until my suspension is lifted. That's it. There will be no love or long-term commitments happening here."

Kevin looked at Isaiah and Will. "Five hundred says he's going to fall for this woman."

The guys glanced at Jacobe, then back at Kevin. Will shook his head. "Nah, I'd rather keep my money."

Isaiah held out his hand. "I'll take that bet. He won't fall, but she will and he's going to drive her away."

Jacobe shook his head and shoved up from the seat. He held out his hand to Kevin. "Make it a thousand. I'm not falling for anyone."

Kevin laughed and slapped hands with Jacobe. "I'll want my money the day after you propose to her."

Danielle returned from her walk on the beach to find Debra standing on the back porch holding two cups from their favorite smoothie place in her hands. Danielle smiled and skipped up the stairs. Debra handed her one of the cups. Danielle took a sip and the delicious flavor of strawberries, blueberries and banana filled her mouth.

"What's bothering you now?" Debra asked.

"Nothing's bothering me. I just needed to get up and move around."

"It's the date with Jacobe, isn't it?"

Debra never let her pretend there wasn't anything wrong. "Why does this have to be about him?"

"Just tell me."

Danielle leaned against the railing of the back porch and took another sip. A breeze ruffled Debra's ponytail, but neither of them made a move toward the back door. The interns were working in the office today. Danielle didn't want them to overhear her silly confusion over her date. That kiss.

"He says he's only volunteering to help his image."

"Which is great. Having him at the gala will bring in tons of money, and possibly even our odds in the upcoming fight with Clear Water, especially if you can convince him to speak up to the council."

"I know, but…"

Debra's brows rose. "But what?"

"I can't really refuse his offer to volunteer. I wouldn't turn anyone away who wants to help. But I just don't want him to think that I'll be so grateful for his help that I'm willing to sleep with him."

"Did he hint around that that's the reason he's helping?"

"No. If anything he made it very clear that his volunteering and his interest in me were two different things."

"And what did you say?"

"That I'm looking for a relationship and not interested in doing the colleagues-with-benefits thing."

"That's a perfect way to make a man run." Debra took a sip of her smoothie. "Did he run away immediately?"

Danielle shifted from one foot to the other. "He kissed me."

Debra almost dropped her smoothie. She caught it

and eyed Danielle. "Well, that's different. So, what, is he interested in you for more than a hookup? I'd think that's what it meant if he kissed you after you said that."

"I have no idea."

"Just think," Debra said, her face bright with excitement. "You could see Jacobe Jenkins in all his tall, muscled glory in your bed."

A vision of naked, glorious Jacobe lying on the flowered sheets in her bed filled her head. Followed by an image of him flicking her lace pillowcases and frowning. She giggled. "It would be a sight to see." She shook her head to clear it of the vision. "I can't go there with him. Making money at the gala and stopping Clear Water are the most important things. As the executive director, I can't turn away having someone as high profile as him bringing attention to our cause. As a woman, I can't afford to sleep with him just because I think he might eventually be interested in a relationship. I've been in love and had the guy leave for bigger and better things."

Debra held the smoothie between her hands and peered at Danielle as if she were analyzing her. Debra's brow raised and her unwavering gaze stayed with Danielle's. "What happened with Luke shouldn't color your future relationships. Don't let fear of not being enough prevent you from trusting your feelings for Jacobe."

"Are you a therapist now?" Danielle groused.

"I'm no therapist, but I have had a lot of therapy. Enough to tell me you want to get closer to him."

Danielle paced back and forth on the porch. "I don't want to get closer to him. I'm curious about him. Something is different about Jacobe. He's still a charmer, still as confident and sexy as ever, but he's holding back. He's not as open anymore. He's been hurt."

"And you can't resist a project."

Danielle's gaze snapped to Debra. "What's that supposed to mean?"

"You like to fix things. That's why you're great at this job." Debra shook her head. "You can't fix a man. Normally, I'd say don't get sucked into trying to figure out what makes him tick and just have a little fun, but that look on your face means if you sleep with him you won't be able to help yourself. Jacobe is sexy, but unless you can really sleep with him without getting your heart involved, stay away. Let him volunteer and help the River Watchers, but send him home alone at the end of the night."

"Is that your professional recommendation?"

Debra nodded. "It is."

Exactly the recommendation Danielle's sensible side gave her. The side that had sent her to a party in college with the hope that Jacobe might be interested said something completely opposite. She'd survived and moved on with just a bruised ego but no major damage to her heart. Could she do the same again?

One night is a lot different from multiple liaisons, the sensible side whispered.

"You're right. I'm going to forget about that kiss and only focus on getting him to help us raise money and beat Clear Water."

"Good," Debra said, pumping her fist in solidarity. "And if you do dabble into the Jacobe pool of temptation, I sincerely hope you prove me wrong."

Danielle hoped the same.

Chapter 6

The auditorium where the Department of Environmental Protection was holding the public hearing on Clear Water's new permit was woefully empty. Danielle scanned the room and caught the familiar faces of the leaders of a few other environmental organizations there, including her River Rat friends, to oppose the new permit and only a few residents of the Crescent Acres community. Public hearings at ten on a Wednesday morning, when most people worked, typically were sparsely attended. Between the staff of Clear Water, the environmental groups and the residents, there were barely twenty people there.

Danielle gritted her teeth. This was one of the most disheartening things about her work. Fighting every day to protect something that people enjoyed using, but getting little to no attention for the cause.

Danielle walked over to the people who'd become the

closest thing she had to family in the area. "Hey, guys," Danielle said to the two ladies and one man.

Mason Kelly lightly bumped her shoulder with his. "Hey, Danielle." His light brown eyes were friendly and he gave her a welcoming smile. He represented the local kayakers in the area. He wore his typical brown hat with a kayak paddle logo over his sandy brown hair, along with cargo shorts and sandals. "Ready to fight today?"

"I can't believe we have to fight this again," Danielle replied.

India Graham nodded. She wore her natural hair in a tapered style that complemented her oval face. "How do you think I feel? I work for Environmental Protection. This is why I need to be in charge of permits. I'd shut these idiots down."

India worked in the monitoring section of the DEP. A section that was slowly getting their resources cut as funding went to other projects. Even though DEP's hesitancy to shut down Clear Water annoyed Danielle, she was thankful there were people who cared like India in the organization.

"Then you better go for a position in permitting when it comes up," Danielle said.

India pointed at Danielle. "Oh, believe me, I am."

Patricia Taylor, the leader of a group who focused specifically on Springfield Creek, sighed. Her curly dark hair was cut short around her plump face and her already tan skin was darker thanks to days working outside. "Depending on how this goes, we may all need to try to work for DEP."

They all nodded. Clear Water had ties to the legislature, who in turn pressured DEP to get their permits approved. Another political battle that they all realized would never end.

"How about drinks later," Danielle said. "Either to celebrate or to drown our sorrows?"

The frown on India's face cleared. "Girl, you just say when and where and I'll be there."

Patricia and Mason agreed. They decided to meet later that day at their favorite bar before taking their seats. India in front with the rest of the DEP staff while she, Mason and Patricia sat on one of the middle rows. Danielle would tell Debra and their group would be set.

The head of the DEP's permit division went to the podium and tapped the microphone. "Thank you for coming. We'll start with a brief overview of the new permit conditions and then we'll ask each person who signed up to speak to come forward. Starting with those in favor of the new permit followed by those against it."

He started going over the main points of the permit. Danielle was already familiar with each one. She looked down at her notes to go over all of her arguments against the department approving the permit.

The man at the microphone stuttered. Danielle glanced up from her notes. The department director was staring at the back of the room, eyes wide. She and the rest of the people turned toward the rear of the auditorium.

"What the hell," Mason muttered to her right.

Danielle's heart fluttered when Jacobe's gaze met hers. He grinned and strolled down the aisle between the rows of metal chairs in her direction, looking confident and casual in a brown button-up and dark pants that flattered his tall body.

The public hearing was more of a regulatory thing, with little possibility of the media showing up, so she hadn't called him to be there on behalf of the River Watchers. Seeing him made her want to bounce with excitement. When he reached her row, he managed to look cool and suave doing the awkward side walk between the chairs to reach her.

"What are you doing here?" she whispered.

He sat next to her, all masculine heat and intoxicating cologne. He leaned in close and studied her with those hot chocolate eyes. "Looking for you."

Mason lightly elbowed her. "You know him?"

"He's volunteering with the River Watchers."

Mason's eyes widened. He turned to Patricia, and they both nodded their heads before looking at Danielle with an *alright now* respect in their eyes. Danielle sat a little taller. Having Jacobe on the River Waters' side was pretty impressive.

The room was still silent as the rest of the occupants, including the director, who was supposed to be moving the hearing along, stared at them wide eyed.

"You're disturbing the peace," she said to Jacobe.

"This is a public hearing. I came to hear what's going on." He glanced at the department director and nodded. "Go ahead."

The director blinked and cleared his throat. "Um… yes, so, as I was saying." He shuffled through his papers and started droning on again.

Danielle glanced around at the sparse crowd now more interested in Jacobe being there than the status of the permit. "You're distracting everyone from the issue," she said so that only he could hear. Well aware Mason was leaning a little closer to eavesdrop.

"I'm curious about the issue, too," he said just as quietly.

"Since when?"

"Since finding out you were here. Debra told me," he said before she could ask.

"Why were you looking for me?"

Knowing that he'd sought her out sent little bubbles of happiness through her chest. "Debra mentioned a cleanup over the weekend. I had a question for you about that."

"She can answer any questions you have."

"Maybe I prefer talking to you." He shifted to spread his long legs as much as he could, which wasn't far into the aisle, and stretched his arms out over the backs of her chair. She became very aware of his arm pressed across the back of her shoulders, and of the curious gazes of her friends on her.

Danielle straightened her glasses and sat forward in the chair. "We're not supposed to be flirting."

Jacobe leaned closer. "I'm not flirting. I'm reaching out to my friend and colleague."

"That's all we are and are going to be," she said, more for her benefit than his.

"That kiss said otherwise."

"A kiss is just that—a kiss. Not a promise for more."

"I understand and respect your decision."

She nodded. He moved his hand over to run his fingers across her upper arm. The barrier of her sweater did nothing to stop the sparks that flew through her body from the soft touch. "That doesn't stop me from thinking about a lot more kisses with you."

Heat spread up her face. She swore she heard Patricia make an *uh oh* sound, but she didn't turn to verify. Instead she swatted his hand away and perched closer to the edge of her seat. "Stop that."

She adjusted her glasses and tried to focus on the front of the room. The director had asked for the proponents of the permit to speak. Danielle tried not to think about Jacobe thinking about kissing her again.

She needed to pay attention to this. The residents affected by this fight deserved her full attention to bring their needs to light. Not for her to spend the entire meeting flirting with Jacobe.

Thankfully, Jacobe didn't say any more and listened to the Clear Water representative speaking at the microphone. The proponents gave the usual argument. Expanding would allow them to handle the excess flow. They were planning massive upgrades to improve treatment. They even pulled out a report by an independent researcher they'd hired who'd said the stream could handle the excess flows they would be discharging—complete with the assurance that only a minimal amount of pollutants, well within the allowance of their permit, would enter the river.

Danielle snorted loud enough to garner some looks with those comments. Patricia and Mason echoed her disbelief. A little pollution from a lot of places added up, and she'd bet money their independent researcher was the same one who'd doctored the numbers in an attempt to show they'd met their permit levels before. Her leg shook with her efforts at restraint—biting her lip instead of calling the representative a liar with each one of his statements.

"And now the opponents," the director said. He glanced at his paper, then looked straight at Danielle. "We'll start with Danielle Stewart, executive director of the St. Johns River Watchers."

Danielle jumped up. Jacobe stood to make it easier for her to slide past him. His body was a strong wall of warm muscle that she couldn't prevent from brushing against as she moved past. Tingles ran through every nerve ending, tingles she forced herself to ignore as she walked to the podium to make her points.

Tingly feelings for Jacobe notwithstanding, she was able to make her argument against allowing the new permit. Her voice rose with her fervor. Fueled by her annoyance at Clear Water's we-aren't-hurting-anyone speech.

"We cannot allow them to pollute Springfield Creek." Danielle slammed her hand on the podium. "Clear Water has failed to eliminate their exceedances for years, and *now* we're supposed to believe they suddenly care. I've brought my own monitoring results that are backed up by the monitoring results made by DEP." She glanced at India, who nodded. "Along with the volunteer monitoring of residents in Crescent Acres. Compare the numbers and you'll find that Clear Water has lied to us again."

She slapped the papers with her monitoring results on the podium. The end of her speech was met with agreements, head nods, and applause from the few people from Crescent Acres who'd attended. The Clear Water representative cringed. Danielle held her chin high and glared at the Clear Water representatives before marching back to her seat.

"You haven't lost that spark," Jacobe said when she was seated again.

"This is important. Other people should realize that." She kept her voice low as the next opponent, a Crescent Acres resident, gave his own impassioned speech.

"You look so sweet and innocent. Then you get up there and rip out their spleens with a few words." He leaned over. "That's incredible sexy." His lips brushed her ear.

Danielle's nipples beaded. She shifted in her chair and tugged on the front of her pink cardigan. Admittedly, people underestimated her zeal and ability to win an argument. She considered that the ace in her pocket. Never a source of sex appeal.

"I don't do it to be sexy."

"Which makes you even sexier." He turned toward the front and listened to the other arguments.

Danielle tried to do the same, but her gaze and attention kept floating back to Jacobe next to her. He watched each of the opponents intently and even nodded his head in agreement with a few of their points. His apparent interest added to his own sex appeal. Debra's warning grew fainter.

"That's the end of the list of people who signed up to speak for or against," the DEP director said. "Thank you all for coming. The comments will be taken into consideration and also posted on the website. The last day for written comments is in four weeks."

The hearing ended. Jacobe placed his hand on Danielle's arm. "Can you send me some of the points you made? I'm thinking of sending in written comments."

"Are you serious?"

"Why do you sound so surprised?"

"You never care about these issues."

"I live on the river a few miles down from this new industry. I had no idea they were dumping upstream from me. I'm going to look into what they're asking for and then decide."

"Oh…sure. I'll send over what I said."

Mason and Patricia hovered at the end of the aisle. The Clear Water proponents watched them with interest. They had to be curious about why Jacobe was there with her.

"Why didn't they do this hearing in the afternoon when more people could come and hear what's happening?"

Danielle shrugged. "That's a question for the state."

He nodded and looked at the department director at the front of the room. "I'll ask them about that. Call me with the details of the cleanup this weekend. I think I'd like to do the one along Springfield Creek." He stood and was so tall her neck strained to keep eye contact. She stood, too, but with flats on he towered over her.

He'd actually looked at the different locations for the cleanups? "You want Springfield Creek?"

"Yeah, it'll get the most publicity if I'm there. I think that makes sense, don't you?"

She'd planned to send him to Springfield Creek for that reason. She wondered if he wanted that location just to help his image or because of what he'd heard today. "I do."

He reached up to brush his fingers across her cheek. "Good." He glanced at her friends. "Introduce me to your friends before I go talk to the director."

Surprisingly, she wanted to say no. Every one of them had seen Jacobe's quick caress of her cheek. They wouldn't say much in front of him, but she'd be grilled at drinks that tonight. "Sure."

He followed her down the aisle to where India, Mason and Patricia stood. She gave quick introductions, which included where they worked. Jacobe smiled and effortlessly charmed her group.

"I really appreciate you all making those comments today," Jacobe said after the conversation lulled. "It gave me a lot to think about. Keep up the good work." He placed a hand on Danielle's lower back. "I'm going to talk to the director now. I'll speak with you soon."

He grinned, then worked his way down the row toward the department director. The Clear Water representatives headed in that way, as well.

Mason placed a hand on her elbow. "How did you get Jacobe Jenkins to volunteer for the River Watchers?"

Danielle shrugged. She wasn't going to admit that he was there because he needed the good publicity. "He just came in asking to help. I couldn't say no."

"You would have been crazy to say no," Patricia said. "Your gala sales will go through the roof."

Exactly what she needed with Liberty breathing down her neck. "I'm just happy to have him participate."

The three kept gushing about how lucky she was to have Jacobe on her team as they walked toward the door. Danielle participated, but her mind kept wandering back to Jacobe. She tried not to think about the meaning behind his touches. He was a flirt. He probably did that without even thinking about it, not because he had any type of feelings for her. She glanced over her shoulder before walking out. Jacobe was watching her, he winked and lifted his chin. Danielle turned away, and pressed her lips together to keep from smiling.

Jacobe had a phone call with his agent, which made him thirty minutes late for the River Watchers cleanup. The call had been worth the extra time. Eric called to give an update on the preliminary talks he'd had with the management of the Phoenix team to gauge their thoughts on Jacobe after the five-game suspension. The talk had gone better than expected. Phoenix would still consider him for their all-star team as long as Jacobe didn't have any more problems this season, which made today's cleanup and the subsequent media attention that much more important.

Groups of people in orange vests were already spread out, picking up litter along the road and in the creek. Danielle stood with a few other volunteers next to a van in the parking lot for the neighborhood's community center, which he guessed was the center of operations.

He'd thought she was sexy earlier that week in the pink sweater that clung to her breasts better than cotton candy on wet fingers. She managed to heat his blood just as much in the khaki pants and dark green shirt she wore today. Her hair was pulled back into a ponytail, and instead of her cute gold glasses she wore a pair of simple black frames. She looked like she was ready to go into battle. Today's battle might be against discarded plastic bottles and trash, but that didn't diminish her fervor.

Jacobe parked in a free space in the parking lot and strolled over to Danielle. "I'm here."

Debra and two of the interns who worked in Danielle's office were the people he'd taken for volunteers when he'd first driven up.

Debra's eyes lit up and she waved. "Jacobe. Great you made it."

He hugged Debra and the two interns. When he turned to hug Danielle, she crossed her arms over her chest and gave him a glower worthy of any five-star general. "You're late."

"I'm sorry. I was on the phone—"

"It's fine." She cut in, waving his words away with her hand. "At least you made it."

"Was there any doubt?"

She cocked a brow, then looked down at the clipboard in her hand. Guess there had been doubt that he'd show up.

He glanced at Debra, who did give him a reassuring glance. "Thanks again for coming out to help."

"I'm happy to," he said. "Where do you want me?"

"Well." Debra glanced at the watch on her wrist.

"I've already broken everyone up into teams and they're out. I'm going with the interns. How about you partner up with Danielle?"

He was more than down with that suggestion. Danielle glared at Debra. Had him being late put her in such a foul mood? She probably thought he was just as inconsiderate of her time now as he had been back in college. True, he was mainly out here to try to improve his image, but after the hearing earlier that week, he did want to know more about the people living around the area. Based on Danielle's impassioned speech, there was a big potential for harm if Clear Water was allowed to discharge into the creek that went through the neighborhood. He wanted to see what was at stake firsthand.

"Sounds like a great plan to me," Jacobe said.

"Fine," Danielle bit out. She slapped the clipboard into Debra's outstretched hand, then turned to grab trash bags and long trash grabbers out of the back of a Jeep. "Let's go pick up at the bridge down there." She pointed in a direction away from most of the volunteers.

"Why down there? You want to be alone with me," he teased, and wiggled his brows.

She didn't smile. "I don't want to distract all the volunteers and take them away from what they're doing by having you nearby. When we meet up back here in about an hour, then they can talk and beg you for an autograph to their heart's content."

"Whatever you think is best."

She spun on her heel and marched toward the bridge. Jacobe looked at Debra, who shrugged. "She's been in a mood all morning."

"What's wrong?"

"I don't know." Debra looked away. Jacobe got the feeling that Debra knew what was bugging Danielle, but he respected that she didn't eagerly divulge her friend's secrets. He'd rather find out from Danielle herself.

He hurried to catch up with Danielle. She didn't even glance his way when he fell into step beside her.

"I wasn't brushing you off or trying to be a jerk when I got here late. My agent called. He had good news for me. I got caught up in that and didn't realize we were on the phone for so long."

"I understand. It's no biggie, really."

She shoved a plastic bag and a stick into his hand and then jerked her head toward the bridge. "Let's go."

"If you were banned from the public hearing earlier this week and one of your board members called to tell you about whether you still had a future with the organization, is there a chance you would have lost track of time?"

She glared at him over her shoulder. "I wouldn't have been banned from a public hearing."

"Humor me, Danielle."

She stopped at the edge of the bridge. The bridge on the two-lane road crossed a small stream that went into the larger creek the rest of the volunteers were cleaning. Even though the bridge was small he eyed the underbrush warily. The vegetation beneath and along the creek bank was thick. The weather was warm. One word crossed his mind: snakes.

Danielle sighed and stabbed at an empty potato chip bag. "I would have listened."

He let go of his concern with snakes to meet her eyes. She'd actually agreed with him. "Since you're the river general I'm sure you would have taken the extra time to talk to your coworker."

One cute arched brow rose. "River general?"

"You lead your troops into battle to protect the river. Sounds right?"

She rolled her eyes but smiled. "That sounds rigid."

"You are rigid."

Her shoulders stiffened. "Not all the time."

Thoughts of her body melting into his when they'd kissed filtered into his brain, warming his insides. "No, not all the time." His voice held whispers of the desire he'd felt that night.

She adjusted her glasses and looked away. "I guess I understand why you were late. I'm sorry for being kind of bitchy when you arrived."

"You know I'm always late."

"Which is so endearing?" She said, sarcasm dripping from every word. She turned and stalked directly into the tall grasses next to the bridge.

"Hey!" He grabbed her arm.

She spun to look at him with wide eyes. "What?"

"You're just going to walk into the grass like that?"

"Um…yeah." She turned to walk, but he didn't let go of her arm.

"Aren't you worried about snakes?"

"Not really," she said, then jerked her arm from his hand. She used the stick to knock the grass out of the way and strolled just as happy as she pleased toward the creek beneath.

Jacobe pushed back a frustrated sigh. Well, if she went down there then he had to go, too. He followed her, his eyes scanning left and right constantly on the lookout for something slithering in the grass. He needed to get his mind off of what might be lurking and focus back on the conversation.

"What was bothering you?" He used his grabber to pick up some of the trash along the way. Danielle moved directly to the water with the single-minded focus of a general.

"I'd hoped we would get some media coverage for this." She made it to the creek bank and began picking up discarded trash with her grabber. "Last year we had two stations show up before the cleanup. No one has shown up this year."

He joined her on the creek bank without coming across any reptiles, but his eyes continued the constant scan for movement. "Did you put in your press release that I was coming?"

"Could you be more conceited?" she asked, elbowing him in the side.

Jacobe laughed and rubbed the spot, though her elbow hadn't hurt. "I'm just saying. Knowing I'm here would do a lot to get attention."

"I appreciate you offering to help out, but I wasn't sure if you'd really show. Getting attention isn't really hard for us for things like this. I figured if they came and you were here it would be a surprise for the media. Plus, I didn't want a bunch of extra *volunteers*," she said, making air quotes with her fingers. "Showing up just to get your autograph instead of actually helping."

Danielle walked closer to the underpass of the bridge. Jacobe once again took a hold of her arm. "Are you sure it's safe to go under there?"

She looked at him like he was crazy. "Do you see the spray paint? Kids hang out under here." She pointed to the graffiti on the cement underpass. "Are you still worried about snakes?"

"I'm trying to figure out why you aren't."

"Running across a snake is common when you work around water. The key is to not panic."

"Who, you or the snakes?"

She laughed, then strolled on beneath the underpass. He should let her go and deal with any snakes she ran across—Ms. Running across a Snake Is Common. He couldn't. If she got hurt when he was around he wouldn't forgive himself. He didn't like getting up close and personal with snakes, but he'd take a bite to protect Danielle.

You've officially lost your mind. What are you now—Tarzan?

He pushed the thought aside. "Why no media?" he asked.

Danielle let out a frustrated sigh and imploded a plastic cup with her grabber. "Council decided to hold a carnival today. That got all the media attention. Normally, I wouldn't care, but one of our board members is on council and I know she pushed to have the carnival on the same day."

"Why would she do that if she's on your board?"

"Because she's only on the board to prove we're keeping the interests of the business sector in mind. I got a lot of attention from council with my campaign against Clear Water last year. She mentioned that the River Watchers is having too much influence in politics that's one-sided. She's not there because she supports our cause."

"Sometimes the businesses have a legitimate argument," he said, sticking close to her as they picked up the litter beneath the bridge. "They can't all be bad."

"I'm not saying they're all bad, but they can try a little harder to protect our natural resources."

Her voice took on the same militant tone she'd used at the public hearing. A tone he'd gotten familiar with in college, which meant she was about to start in on a passionate speech. He didn't mind when Danielle's passion came out. He just preferred to have her passion surface in his bed rather than beneath a bridge.

"So the media was a no-show," he said before she could start. "I get that's annoying, but they might still send someone out. It seemed like there was a little more to your funk than that?"

"My...funk?" She grinned at him.

"You know you act funky when you're in a mood. Wrinkling up your cute little nose like you've smelled something bad."

She touched her nose. He had a strong urge to push her hand aside and kiss her. But, again, kisses were for better places than snake-hiding bridges.

"What's bothering you?"

She dropped her hand. Turning away from him, she sighed and grabbed more trash for her bag. Her bag was halfway full, and so was his. Jacobe took in all the litter in the small section of creek near the bridge. Driving over this road, he never would have realized there was that much trash out here.

"My parents were supposed to come to the cleanup today." Danielle wasn't looking at him.

"Do they typically come?"

"No. They typically promise to attend one of my events and not show up." Her tone rang with the false cheerfulness of someone who'd been let down often but didn't want to admit their feelings were hurt.

"I'm sorry."

"Don't be. If I'm a general, then my parents are admirals in the fight against social injustice. They've got more important things to worry about."

The hurt in her voice tugged at something inside of him. Something that made him want to pull her into his arms until the hurt went away. "More important than supporting their daughter?"

"I shouldn't expect to come first when there are so

many people in the world that deserve attention more than me."

The words sounded rehearsed. He had a feeling she'd repeated the phrase hundreds of times. Whether to convince herself or others was what he wanted the answer to.

"Has anyone ever put you first?"

Her lips and the corners of her eyes tightened. "I put myself first."

"Do you? You're always fighting other battles."

"I fight important battles. I bring attention to things that affect people who would otherwise be ignored. No one deserves to be ignored or left behind. What battles do you fight?"

Her words pierced him. The anger in her voice made him freeze. He'd left her behind.

She walked toward a plastic bag near the other side of the bridge. Jacobe knew it wasn't his imagination. There was definitely something long, dark and snake-like beneath that bag.

"Danielle, wait!" He rushed over and jerked her behind him. In one quick swoop, he pushed the bag aside and used his grabber to fling the snake into the water.

"What are you doing?" she asked.

He spun to face her. "Saving you from a snakebite." Now that the moment was over he realized what he'd done. He hated snakes. They were the one thing he was afraid of, and he'd pushed her aside to face it himself. A surge of masculine pride puffed up his chest.

Tarzan, huh?

He looked at Danielle. Ready to soak in her awe and feminine gratitude for him coming to her rescue. Danielle's eyes sparkled with laughter and her hand covered her mouth.

"What? Did you see what I just did?"

She pointed to the water. "You saved me from a piece of inner tube."

He glanced in the direction she pointed. Sure enough, a piece of inner tube floated downstream. No sign of a snake anywhere.

"Well, damn," he said, and glanced at her. He joined in her laughter.

"I appreciate the attempt, though." Her smile softened. "And I'm sorry about that earlier comment. My parents not showing is kind of a touchy subject for me. I shouldn't have taken it out on you."

"I may not have called you, but I never forgot you. Don't ever forget that."

The humor and apology in her eyes shifted into something else. Something warm and inviting that had him taking a step toward her. To hell with the thought that kissing beneath a bridge was a bad idea. He was about to thoroughly kiss Danielle Stewart.

He reached out for her, his hand grazing her waist. She didn't pull back. A crackling noise interrupted the moment. Jacobe frowned and looked around.

Danielle stepped back and reached for the walkie-talkie on her hip. "Go ahead, Debra." Her voice trembled slightly.

"There's a reporter here who wants to conduct an interview and get more information about the cleanup."

Danielle's grin brought sunshine to the dark space they were in. "I'll be right there."

"See," Jacobe said. "I told you the news would show up."

Her eyes narrowed in on him suspiciously. "Did you have anything to do with this?"

"I may have asked my agent to call a few stations when I was on my way out here. I am here to show people I'm cleaning up my act." Though he now wished he'd asked Eric to call just to make Danielle smile like that.

They backtracked back to the Jeep, where the interns and Debra were. Many of the other volunteers were around and the buzz of excitement grew when they recognized him. Jacobe was happy to greet the volunteers, many of them teenagers and families who lived in the area. He snapped selfies that he knew would hit social media and spread the word faster than any interview the reporter completed.

"Do you want to talk to the reporter?" Danielle asked while the journalist set up his camera on a tripod.

"This is your event. You talk first."

He watched Danielle handle with ease the questions the reporter threw her way. She used the same confident tone, and he was learning to love that about her.

One of the teens volunteering came over. "I just want to thank you."

Jacobe shook the young man's hand. "I'm happy to come out and help. I care about our waterways."

"Not that," the kid said. "I'm in the Big Brother program. My mentor told me that you're a big sponsor. I just want you to know that I appreciate that. It's helped me a lot."

"I don't do that for the attention," Jacobe said. "But I'm glad it's helping someone. Do you live out here?"

"Yeah. It's why I volunteered. Me and my little brother used to play in this creek a lot when we were kids. My granddad used to fish out here. Gotta take care of your home, ya know."

Jacobe thought about what would happen if Clear Water's permit went through. Would it be safe for kids to play in the water, for families to fish? *"I bring attention to things that affect people who would otherwise be ignored."*

Jacobe patted the boy on his back. "You do. Keep up the good work?"

"I'll try."

Danielle called him over then. Jacobe patted the teen on the shoulder and went to do his interview. Two other stations showed up and also interviewed him, Danielle and the various volunteers. Jacobe had planned to give a canned response about doing his part and showing that he cared. Instead, he talked about the importance of protecting Springfield Creek for the kids who played in it every day. He didn't speak out directly against Clear Water—he needed more information before doing that—but he was no longer sure he could remain neutral in this publicity stunt.

The look of feminine adoration on Danielle's face that he'd expected when going up against the innertube snake was there after his interview. It sent a twist through his chest that made him want to come back next weekend and do the same.

The reporters went off to get a few shots of the volunteers picking up litter and the mountains of bags they collected.

"Thank you for that," Danielle said. "I didn't think you would sound so sincere in your efforts."

"Neither did I. I guess you're rubbing off on me just a little."

She laughed. "Doubtful."

"How are we going to celebrate a successful cleanup?"

"Debra and I usually take some of the volunteers out for lunch afterward. On Monday, I'll crunch the numbers and then when I get the weight of the trash from the landfill I'll send out word to the volunteers and our board."

He shook his head. "No, we've got to do something a lot more fun than that."

Debra came over and wrapped an arm around Danielle's shoulders. "Did I hear the word *fun*?"

"You did," Jacobe said. "I was just telling Danielle that we need to celebrate a successful cleanup."

"Beers over lunch is good," Danielle said.

"Shush, woman," Debra said. "A handsome and successful professional basketball player is offering to throw us a party. Don't ruin it."

Jacobe laughed. "I was thinking more along the lines of taking you guys out on my yacht. You're doing so much to protect the waterways, why not enjoy it."

The thought had just popped into his mind. He wanted another date with Danielle but knew she would find an excuse to say no. A trip on the water with her key staff would allow him to talk to her more and give them a treat for the good work they were always doing.

"You've got a yacht?"

"Not a big one, but yes, I do. Me and the guys go out deep-sea fishing every once in a while. I'll take you and the staff out. You can invite a board member or two, as well." He put emphasis on the words *board member*. He wanted to meet this person trying to snatch his general's stars.

"Yes!" Debra answered.

Danielle didn't look quite as convinced. He grinned at her. "Come on, Danielle. Even generals have to relax every now and then."

She studied first Debra, then him. He could see the yes in her eyes before she said, "Okay, fine. We'll treat the staff to a trip."

Chapter 7

Jacobe checked and double-checked the weather forecast the following Wednesday, when he'd agreed to take Danielle and the rest of the crew from the River Watchers out on his yacht. Today, the meteorologist had given a dead-on forecast. The day was sunny and beautiful seventy-six degrees with only a few clouds in the sky. All morning images of Danielle on deck in a skimpy bikini had danced in his head.

When she, Debra and four of the River Watchers interns arrived at the marina his hopes were dashed. Danielle wore a loose pair of jeans rolled up around her slim ankles and a dark blue crew-neck T-shirt. A thick blue-and-cream-striped sweater hung over her arm. She was covered from head to toe, but that didn't diminish how happy he was to see her.

"Right on time," he said to her and Debra.

Debra and the interns were equally covered in T-shirts, jeans or khakis, but he could see the straps of swimsuits beneath their shirts. He peeked at Danielle's neckline, but didn't see a bathing-suit strap around her neck.

"We always are," Danielle said. She glanced around. "I thought you lived on the river. You don't keep your boat at your home?"

"I keep her stored here for the winter and most of the year. This is the first time I've taken her out this year. When the season's over, I'll bring her to my personal dock if I know I'll go out a lot more." He glanced at Debra. "You all can go on up. My girl is the *Freedom*. I hope you don't mind, but I invited Kevin and Isaiah. Will couldn't make it. They're already on board."

A murmur of excitement went through the interns. Debra's eyes lit up. "We don't mind at all."

Debra and the interns headed down the pier to where his boat was anchored. Danielle had stuck behind, as he'd hoped. He wanted a few minutes alone with her.

"Anyone else coming?" he asked.

"I invited the board president and vice president. They've agreed."

"Is one of them the council member?"

Her hair was held back by a dark blue headband and hung to just below her chin. The breeze had blown a few strands into her eyes. He fought the urge to reach out and push them away.

"Yes, the vice chair of council and president of my board is Liberty Myers. I also invited Mr. Springfield."

"Springfield? Is the creek named after him?"

"Not him, his family. The Springfield family owned much of the land around the creek for decades. Clear Water's discharge, if the permit is approved, will go through his land, too. He has an interest in preventing the permit, as well."

She shifted on her feet and tugged at her bra strap beneath her shirt. Maybe it wasn't a bra strap? Hope that he would still get to see her in a bikini sprang in his chest. "Do you think she knows that she's invited so I can change her mind?"

Danielle shook her head. Her arms crossed beneath her breasts, pushing them up. Jacobe's eyes dipped. He forced them back up. He wasn't an adolescent. He wouldn't stare at her like he couldn't wait to see what was beneath her T-shirt.

"As board president, it makes sense for me to invite her on a trip set up as a reward for the River Watchers. I wouldn't come on too strong, though."

"I like coming on strong." He took a step toward her. Jacobe ran his finger along the edge of her glasses.

"You're also very persistent. Jacobe, I meant what I said on our date."

Those were words that should have made him take a step back. Words that should remind him that Danielle wanted a relationship. Relationships required trust, and he wasn't ready to trust anyone again.

"I know what you want, Danielle." He ran his fingers down her cheek and neck, stopping at the rapid beat of her pulse at the base of her throat. "I also want you."

A line formed between her brows. Dozens of questions floated in her warm brown eyes. "What does that mean?"

"Exactly what I said. I want you."

Voices and footsteps drew nearer. Jacobe dropped his hand and took a step back. He looked in the direction of the noise and saw a man and woman approach. The woman appeared to be in her early forties. Her dark brown hair was pulled back into a ponytail and she wore shorts and a T-shirt. The man was older, fifties, if Jacobe guessed, with graying hair. He too was dressed casually for a day on the water.

They spotted Danielle and Jacobe. The woman smiled and waved before they both walked toward him and Danielle.

"Hello, Danielle. Jacobe Jenkins," the woman said, holding out her hand. "I'm Liberty Meyer and this is Jeff Springfield. It is a pleasure to meet you."

Jacobe shook her hand. "Pleasure meeting you, as well. Danielle has told me how much the board has supported her efforts as the director of the River Watchers. I insisted that we invite you to show our appreciation."

Liberty's eyes shifted to Danielle, then back to him. "We?"

"Danielle and I are good friends. We've known each other since college. I've always been impressed by her passion for bringing attention to causes that are easily ignored."

Jeff nodded in agreement. "Danielle is the perfect person for the job. She is very dedicated."

Danielle adjusted her glasses. "I just try to do what's right."

Jacobe rubbed her back. She stiffened slightly but didn't pull away. She was lucky rubbing her back was all he'd done. He wanted to pull her against him as if they really were a couple. "Not many people are willing to fight for what they believe in. Come on aboard. I'll let the captain know we're ready."

They went aboard and Jacobe left Danielle with her people and his teammates to give the captain the instructions. Not long after they were heading to sea. He turned on music. He preferred old-school hip-hop, but with the mixed crowd he opted for the new music his friend Dante Wilson was putting out. A fusion blend of classical, hip-hop and jazz. He'd been skeptical of the idea of the fusion mix when he'd first learned about it, but after hearing the music Dante and his group, Strings A Flame, were making, Jacobe had become a fan.

He'd ordered food for the daytime excursion since they planned to be out for most of the day. They stopped about twenty miles offshore and dropped the anchor. That's when Kevin and Isaiah mentioned Jet Skis and swimming. The group congregated on the back deck. Debra and the interns and even Liberty and Jeff quickly stripped down to bathing suits and life jackets, and jumped on the Jet Skis.

Danielle opted out of getting in the water and sat in one of the leather seats and watched. Jacobe chose to stay with her while everyone else played. She had stealthily avoided him while they were heading out to sea, talking with his teammates, Debra, the interns or board members. He guessed she was trying to figure out what he'd meant. He was trying to figure that out, too. He wanted her, but how much was he willing to surrender himself to in order to have her.

When he sat beside her close enough for their legs to brush, she quickly scooted away. "Not going out with the rest of them?" he asked.

"Okay, don't laugh, but I'm afraid of getting on a Jet Ski."

He drew back with exaggerated shock. "The river general is afraid of a Jet Ski. You go under snake-infested bridges without batting an eye, but you're afraid of a Jet Ski?"

She laughed and hit his arm. "The bridge wasn't snake infested. It was inner-tube infested."

"They look the same."

"No, they don't."

He shifted closer. "We'll agree to disagree. Why don't you do Jet Skis?"

"I fell off a Jet Ski once in college and haven't gotten on another since."

"How did that happen?"

She shrugged. "Went to the lake with some friends. My boyfriend took off before I was ready and—splash, I fell off, and he zoomed on."

Jacobe's ears perked up at the mention of a boyfriend. His anger rose, too, with the thought of the guy leaving her behind. "Sounds like a jerk."

She shook her head. "Not at all. That was nothing but a lack of communication. He immediately turned around and scooped me out of the water. I was fine, but a bit frightened. Neither of us got back on the Jet Ski and spent the rest of the day chilling on the beach."

The nostalgic smile on her face, full of sweet remembrance of a fond memory, made his stomach clench in knots. Jealousy? Really?

"You liked that guy?" He hoped she didn't say the ex-boyfriend's name. Without a name, he didn't seem quite real.

"I did." Her brows drew together, then she looked out over the water at the group cheering and playing.

He wondered what that frown was about, but he wasn't interested in hearing any more stories about an ex-boyfriend. "Come on the Jet Ski with me."

"No, thank you. I'd rather not find myself plunged into the middle of the ocean."

He laughed. "You won't. If you prefer, I'll get behind you and hold on. You can plunge *me* into the middle of the ocean if you prefer."

"You can be annoying," she said with a grin. "But I don't want you to fly off the back of a Jet Ski."

"It'll be fun. Come on, let's try."

She watched the others and bit her lip. "Give me a second to think about it, okay?"

"Sure." He slid closer to her on the seat. She didn't notice and didn't move away. "That time in college— was it the first time you'd ridden one?"

"No. After Hurricane Fabian in 2003, my parents and I traveled to Bermuda to help with efforts to restore the coastline. My dad took me out on one once during that vacation."

"Sounds like a fun vacation," he said, not bothering to hide his sarcasm.

"Actually, it was fun. It was the first time I'd gone anywhere with just me and my parents that I can remember."

"You traveled with others a lot?"

"There were always other people around my parents. I'm an only child, but my parents always busy with other things. There are so many people who need help in the world, it's only right that they answer the call."

Her words had that rehearsed sound he'd heard before when she'd tried to hide that she was upset they hadn't come to the cleanup. The sound of someone used to being forgotten.

"When the opportunity to help after the hurricane came up, Dad signed us up to go. We helped rebuild the coastline and even worked on a few houses during the day. Sometimes, we got the chance to just hang out, but there was so much work to be done. Dad rented a Jet Ski and took me out. We had so much fun, laughing and going fast. Mama nearly had a heart attack."

"That does sound fun." No sarcasm. "Did you go out a lot on the Jet Ski?"

"No. It was just that afternoon. There were too many other things to be done. The best vacations are ones where you're giving back."

He stretched out his legs and rested his arm behind her. The position allowed him to brush his thumb across her shoulder. He liked touching her. "To me, the best vacations are the ones where you do nothing but relax and have sex."

Her eyes snapped to his and she sucked in a breath. "What?"

"Exactly what I said."

She frowned. "That's not the point of a mission trip."

"Maybe not, but I'd find the time. I'd also make sure I planned vacations that are about nothing but having fun. If you spend all of your free time giving to others without doing something for yourself eventually you run out of things to give."

She looked away and sat up so he couldn't touch her. "That's a selfish thought."

"No, it's a true statement. We all have to relax and recharge. The world won't end if you take a second to just enjoy it."

"I was raised to believe it's the responsibility of every person on this planet to do what they can to make it a better place."

The general's voice again. "Really, so what's your dream vacation, then?"

She looked sheepish. "You're going to think I'm crazy, but there's this group that provides water-purification systems and builds wells for people who don't have access to clean drinking water around the world. I'd love to volunteer and go with them one year."

Jacobe sat up straight and pulled back his hand. Not because he disliked her idea but because her dream vacation was so noble. So damn honorable that it reminded him that he should walk away and stop pursuing her. She deserved better than the friend-with-benefits relationship he was able to give.

"You think I'm crazy, don't you?"

Jacobe took her hand in his and squeezed gently. "No. I actually think you're amazing." He looked into her eyes. "I admire your passion, and your compassion. But, can we at least agree that it's also the right of every person to take care of themselves, as well? Having a little fun, without guilt, isn't the end of the world. You know that. You've done that before."

A low blow. He didn't care. Right now he wanted the little bit daring, little bit wild Danielle who'd come to a party that night in college to come out for a little while.

"That night was…"

"A mistake?" He really hoped that wasn't what she was going to say.

She shook her head. "No. It was the only time I did something truly reckless and just because I wanted it. Because I wanted you."

"The world didn't end, and as you said, you moved on."

"Not easily, but I did." She whispered the words, then pulled her lip between her teeth.

He squeezed her hand again, fought the urge to pull her in close and kiss her. There were too many people on the boat. Too many people who had no reason to not tell the world that he'd kissed her. He normally didn't care who knew about the women he slept with, but he wanted whatever happened between him and Danielle to be between the two of them. Just like their night in college had been. Their own sweet secret.

"Ride the Jet Ski with me?" he asked. He needed something to do besides sit there and try not to kiss her.

She glanced at the group on the water, then back at him. "Okay. Let's do it."

Danielle had avoided getting on a Jet Ski ever since Luke dropped her into the lake back in college, but fear of falling off wasn't what caused her insides to flutter as she settled into the seat. The searing heat in Jacobe's eyes when she'd stripped of her jeans and shirt was the reason. Appreciation followed by the thorough inspection he'd given as she removed her outer layers made her feel like she was wearing the sexiest of bikinis instead of the sporty blue-and-black two-piece.

Before she could get a good grip on the gears, Jacobe sat down behind her, and wrapped her with the heat from his body. The inside of his legs pressed tightly against hers. The firm muscles of his chest were flush against her back, and his oh-so-long and strong arms wrapped snugly around her waist.

There was no way she should feel his body heat between two layers of life jackets, yet he seemed to burn into her flesh. Her mind had to be playing tricks on her.

He leaned forward. "You good?" His lips brushed her ear.

She tensed and gripped the handles. Jacobe ran one hand up and down her arm while the other squeezed her in what she guessed was a hug from behind. "It's okay, I won't let you fall."

Falling was not where her head was at right now. She cleared her throat and nodded. "I'm good. Just getting comfortable."

"Am I holding you too tight?"

He could hold her a lot tighter and she'd be cool. "Uh...nah. You're fine. You sure you don't mind being behind me?"

His hands gripped her waist and he pulled her farther into the crook of his legs. Heat shot through Danielle's body, and she fought not to twist backward in his embrace. "I'm loving this position."

His voice sounded thicker. She didn't dare glance over her shoulder to see if the look in his eye matched. His sexy voice and hot looks were all well and good when they were on the boat, not so much when his hands could singe into the bare skin of her hips and thighs and his very essence surrounded her.

"You ready?" he asked.

She nodded. The sooner she started the sooner this ended. "Let's do this."

Debra clapped from the back of the boat. "Have fun, Danielle."

Danielle shot her friend a glare, then laughed when Debra wiggled her eyebrows.

"Hold on." She twisted the controls and they shot forward.

Why had she told him to hold on? One hand stayed on her hip, and the other wrapped around her waist. He moved with her in perfect harmony. His body melding to hers as she zipped and streamed through the water. The Jet Ski hummed beneath her, but that was nothing compared to the vibrations going through her body. Despite the mist of water that hit them, she felt overheated, burning with a need to get closer to Jacobe.

Jacobe moved his arms from around her waist. One hand clasped her shoulder, and the other pressed against her upper thigh. His fingers trailed up to her hip then back down where he squeezed. Danielle's grip jerked and the Jet Ski lurched forward. His arm shot around her waist and he held her tighter than before.

"All right?" he asked.

Her heart thudded. "Yeah, I'm going back in now." She yelled over her shoulder and made her way back toward the yacht.

When they returned, she quickly took Kevin's outstretched hand and hurried off the Jet Ski. She didn't wait for Jacobe to get off as she hurried onto the deck.

A few seconds later, Jacobe lightly touched her arm. "Are you okay?"

She spun around and stepped out of his reach. Concern filled his eyes and he moved closer to her.

"Yeah, maybe it was all the jostling around, but I feel a little light-headed." A lame excuse, but she needed a second to compose herself.

Liberty walked over. For the first time in a long time, Danielle was happy when the woman interrupted her.

"You two sure looked like you had a good time," Liberty said. She held a small plate of shrimp cocktail in her hand.

Jacobe glanced at Danielle. "I always have fun hanging with Danielle."

Sharp curiosity filled Liberty's gaze. "Do you two hang out a lot?"

Danielle shook her head, but Jacobe spoke. "More so recently with the proposed permit for Clear Water. I live on the river and some of the boys in the mentoring program I sponsor live in Crescent Acres. We'll all be affected if their permit goes through."

Danielle had to give him props. He'd eased the conversation to the permit easily. But, then again, Jacobe had always been smooth.

"You're following the Clear Water situation?" Liberty sounded surprised.

"I am. Closely. Not just the situation with the possible pollution, but can the creek even handle the excess flows? I mean, it's a decent size, but will the extra water cause flooding of properties along the bank in larger rains?"

Danielle's and Liberty's jaws dropped. Liberty was too busy watching Jacobe to notice Danielle's shock, which gave Danielle the chance to snap her mouth shut. For him to bring that up meant he had to have done more research on his own. The point had been minor in her speech during the public hearing. She got a giddy, glowing feeling in the pit of her stomach, along with a tightening of her skin and an overwhelming urge to grin uncontrollably. There could only be one reason.

She was starting to like Jacobe. Not just like him as a sponsor and ally, but *like* like him. Like him as she would a guy she wanted to date.

Because you do want him. You want him bad.

Danielle swayed slightly, the thought an unwanted shock to her system. She did not need to fall for a man who clearly said he wasn't looking for a serious relationship.

He instantly looked her way and put a hand on her arm. "Are you okay?"

She nodded, but couldn't meet his eyes. The giddy, I-could-fall-for-this-guy feeling hadn't gone away. "I'm going to sit for a second. I think it's a combination of the ride and being on the water for so long. You two keep talking."

He didn't let her arm go. "Do you need to lie down?"

"No. Just a few seconds to settle my brain." She met his dark sexy eyes. Heat flooded her face.

Jacobe frowned. Maybe he saw that she was on the verge of losing it. "Come with me. Excuse us, Liberty."

He took her hand and led her into the cabin, then down into the bowel of the ship.

"Seriously, I'm fine."

"Just trust me. It's much quieter down here. Besides, you look as if you're about to pass out."

They went down a wood-paneled hall and into another room.

Danielle took one look at the queen-sized bed and her heart jumped in her chest. She did not need to be alone in a bedroom with Jacobe. "What are you doing?"

"Lie down for a few minutes. Take as long as you need. I'll go back up." He released her hand and went over to the bed, where he moved the covers. "The bathroom's in there. I think there's some antinausea medicine in there and something for a headache. Don't worry about falling asleep, I'll check on you in about thirty minutes if you're not back up."

He returned to stand in front of her. His concerned gaze studied her. She was a sucker for a man who cared.

He made a move toward the door. Danielle grabbed his arm. "You're really concerned about me?"

"I shouldn't have insisted that you ride the Jet Ski. I didn't think about you not feeling okay after you got off."

"I'm someone who doesn't like to be blindsided, and you're doing that to me."

He frowned. "I don't understand."

"You're being thoughtful and considerate. Not to mention talking to Liberty as if you really care."

"I do care." He sounded a little annoyed that she'd implied otherwise.

The fluttery feeling, the one she needed to ignore,

intensified. "I'm...impressed. I didn't know what to think when you brought me down here."

He shifted back and eyed her warily. "You didn't think I would bring you down here for something else if you're not feeling well."

Danielle shook her head and waved a hand. "No. I just didn't realize you could be so sweet."

"Don't let the word get out. Some people take sweetness for weakness." A hint of cynicism entered his voice.

"Is that what Christy did?"

His body went rigid. "Something like that. Look, I'll leave you alone."

He tried to move away and again she held on to his arm. "I'm sorry. I said I wouldn't bring that situation up again."

"I know your intent isn't malicious."

"I'm sorry that she hurt you."

"Finding out that the child I thought was mine really wasn't came with a bit of pain." His face and voice were impassive, but she felt the hurt that accompanied the rigid tension of his body.

Danielle took a step forward and placed her hand on his chest. His heart beat wildly beneath the wall of muscle. "She sounds like a bitch."

Jacobe's eyes widened. The tension in his body evaporated. "Did the river general really just call another woman a bitch?"

"I'm sorry, but for her to treat you that way, to lie to you like that. There's no other word for it."

Jacobe shifted close until only her hand separated their bodies from touching. She was tempted to pull it away. "Danielle, let me apologize right now."

"For what?"

"I'm about to be anything but sweet." He gripped her hips and lifted her off her feet. Danielle gasped and grabbed onto his shoulders. He wrapped an arm around her waist to hold her against him.

"Just because I called her that?"

"That, and a little bit because of your bikini."

"It's sporty, not sexy."

He shifted her higher, nudging her forward with the movement. "Everything you wear is sexy." He kissed her.

She went with instinct. Her arms wrapped around his neck, and her legs circled his torso. Kissing would not help her get over the crazy feeling that she wanted to take a risk and be with Jacobe, yet there was no way she would stop.

In two swift steps, he had her across the room. A second later, her back met the cool sheets on the bed. Danielle opened to him. His large body pressed her deep into the soft mattress. The smell of the ocean, clean sheets and Jacobe drugged her. The heat of his skin over the play of firm muscles ignited her even more. Her short nails dug into his shoulders.

Jacobe gripped her hips and settled his firmly between hers. The insistent press of his erection pushed against the flimsy material of her bathing suit. The thick length rubbed enticingly against her dampening core. He rocked his hips. The ridge of his cock slid against the most sensitive spot on her body.

Danielle gasped and her head pressed back. Pleasure slipped over her body like silk. Jacobe pulled her lower lip between his, before deepening the kiss. She grabbed his shoulders. Pulled him closer. Jacobe's achingly thorough kiss was a sweet, intimate caress that slowly intensified her desire. One hand gripped the hair on his head, holding him tight. The other ran across the strength of his back. His hips continued to slowly push back and forth, winding her body tighter and tighter, pressure building in her midsection with each movement.

He broke the kiss to lick and suck along her chin, neck and torso. One of his hands cupped her breast. His fingers playing with the hard nub of her nipple.

"Damn, Danielle, you smell so good." He groaned into her neck. The tip of his tongue flicked against her neck. "Taste so damn good." His hips rotated again.

Danielle bucked, her fingers clinging to his head as he tasted her. "Jacobe," she moaned.

"If we were alone on this boat I'd strip this damn bikini off of you and taste every part of you. I still remember what you tasted like. Do you remember the way I licked you?" His tongue leisurely explored across her neck.

Did she remember? Was the ocean salty? He'd spread her legs wide that night so long ago. Spread her open and savored her for what felt like hours even though it was only a few rushed minutes. She hadn't lasted long. Had climaxed almost immediately around his expert tongue. Then he'd kissed her, and she'd been helpless to do anything but tear his shirt open and push his pants down in a frenzy to get more of him.

"Oh, you remember." The male satisfaction in his voice only melted her bones more.

Danielle pulled his head back up for another kiss. Memories of that night fused with the delicious imprint of his body on top of hers. She wanted more, needed more.

He reached down, rearranged himself until the full ridge of his erection pushed firmly against her swollen nub. His hips moved in deliberate, firm thrusts.

The movement was both delicious and maddening. She wanted her bottoms off, his swim trunks gone and his body thick and deep inside of her. The image of him was so clear, the memory of their time together so real, that her body tightened. Her mouth opened to beg for more when her world exploded. Pleasure burst through every filament of her being. Her legs clenched around his waist.

Her shout was cut off by his mouth over hers. He kissed her deeply, slowly, as she eased back to reality. All too soon the reality of what had just happened set in. Her cheeks burned and embarrassment slammed through her.

"Oh, my God, I can't believe we just did that," she said between pants. She felt his gaze but kept her eyes firmly closed. She could only imagine what he thought. How uneventful her love life had to be for her to orgasm so easily. "We shouldn't have done that. We're just supposed to be working together. We're—"

He cut her off with a quick brush of his lips across hers. "Worry about what we just did tomorrow, okay. Today is about having fun."

"I know, but we shouldn't have—"

"Danielle, I'm still between your legs with a pretty uncomfortable hard-on, and you're already telling me this was a mistake."

"Oh. I'm sorry. Do you want me to do something?" All the eagerness she'd felt earlier was gone, replaced with mortification and regret.

He shook his head. "No, you can stay. I'll need a few minutes to get...myself straight. If you know what I mean."

"What does this mean?"

"Let's not analyze that right now. Okay?"

Not exactly what she wanted to hear, though not a surprise, either. He'd already said he wasn't ready for a committed relationship. Of course, he wouldn't want to analyze getting her off with just a slow grind. More heat flushed her cheeks. "You're right. I'm sorry. You stay. I'll go back up."

"If that's what you want."

They stared at each other. His erection was not decreasing an inch. "You need to get off me."

"Yeah. Right." He pushed away from her in a rush. His gaze roamed over her on the bed before his lips pressed together in a thin line. He rearranged the bulge in his shorts and turned away. "I'll be up in a minute."

Danielle jumped off the bed and scurried to the door. "Take your time. You know, finishing—"

"Goodbye, Danielle." His voice was strained, almost angry. She hurried out and back up to the deck.

Debra came over immediately. "What's wrong? Liberty said you were sick. Where's Jacobe? Did he give you something?"

Danielle gripped Debra's arm. "Not now, Debra. I'm good."

Debra's gaze sharpened. A second later her jaw dropped and she leaned in. "Did you?"

Danielle shook her head. "No!" she said in a harsh whisper. "Not. Now."

Debra waved a hand. "Fine. Not now, but later." Her eyes sparked with interest.

Danielle's face burned so hot she was surprised smoke didn't rise from her cheeks. There was no way she could tell the story of how humiliating it was to get off from a fully clothed, slow grind.

Chapter 8

Leading the Gators to a twenty-point win in New York was the pièce de résistance at the end of Jacobe's five-game suspension. He leaned back and stretched his arms over the back of the leather couches in Mahogany, the swank uptown nightclub owned by Calvin Rush, a connection Jacobe had made through his friend, movie star Irvin Freeman. Isaiah sat on the leather chair to Jacobe's right, and buckets of champagne and empty glasses covered the marble table in front of him in the VIP section.

He normally enjoyed clubbing after a game but was having a hard time finding his groove tonight. If he didn't let off some steam he was likely to burst. His gaze roamed the crowded club, taking in all the beautiful ladies. Any one of them could help release the pressure building inside. Ever since Danielle had walked away last Saturday, he'd had a semi hard-on that only seemed to disappear when he played ball.

Frustration pounded through him with every beat of his heart. Not because she'd walked away—he'd never push her into anything she didn't want to do—but because she'd immediately regretted what happened the second after she'd climaxed.

And her climax had been something to behold. The way her small hands clutched his shoulders while her slim legs wrapped around his hips. The way her dark eyes had gone out of focus and rolled to the back of her head. The sexy sweep of her tongue over her lower lip. Her body jerking and bucking beneath him.

Jacobe groaned and reached for the glass of champagne on the table. Damn, he had to get her out of his mind. He'd been in a one-sided relationship before. If her first thought when they were in that position was that they'd made a mistake, then obviously she was still unsure about moving forward with him. That should be good. He knew he wasn't ready for anything serious. That didn't mean he wanted her to regret it if their relationship naturally progressed physically.

He needed to move on. He wouldn't get caught up in a woman who wasn't ready to acknowledge the heat simmering between them. Tonight, he was going to celebrate being back on the court and the team's win with one of the beautiful women in the place.

Kevin walked up with three beauties surrounding him. It was divine intervention telling Jacobe he was on the right path.

"Ladies, let me introduce you to my teammates. Jacobe and Isaiah. Fellas, these beautiful ladies are Teresa, Nicole and Davina," Kevin said, pointing to each of the women as he introduced them.

Davina, a sexy brunette with tan skin and attractive green eyes sat next to Jacobe. The edges of her tight black dress rode up her toned thighs and the light scent of her perfume surrounded him. "Congratulations on your win." Her voice was like warm honey.

"Thank you," Jacobe said. He shifted away to give her more room on the couch, but she followed his movement, plastering her curvaceous body against his side. "Are you a fan?"

"Of basketball, no. Of you, most definitely." Her hand played along his thigh.

Jacobe waited for the arousal that had nagged him from the moment he'd left Danielle to take over his body. His body said yes. This is what he needed. This was what he should be doing. On a physical level he was fully capable of accepting what Davina had to offer. His brain on the other hand was hesitant. He could take Davina back to his hotel room, but he wouldn't be satisfied. The desire pushing at him from the inside wouldn't go away. Davina wasn't the woman that had caused the buildup.

"Excuse me, I'm going to get a drink." He pushed Davina's hand off his thigh and stood. Ignoring her gasp of surprise and Kevin's knowing smirk, Jacobe left the VIP section and headed to the bar.

Calvin stood at the edge of the bar talking to one of the bartenders. Calvin was quiet and mostly kept to himself, but Jacobe liked him. Calvin always found a table for Jacobe when he popped in, and he had let him leave through a secret exit once when Jacobe had wanted to avoid the paparazzi.

"Calvin, what are you doing hanging out at the bar?" Jacobe and Calvin clasped hands.

Calvin moved to the side to give Jacobe more room at the bar. "I like to come out and check on things every once in a while. I don't spend the entire night in my office."

"You really aren't enjoying all the perks of owning one of the hottest clubs in New York. If you let these women know who you were you'd have most of them trying to take you home tonight."

Calvin chuckled but shook his head. "Not interested in taking anyone here home. Too much of a chance they'd come back angry when things didn't work out. Speaking of which, why did you leave a beautiful woman to come hang out at the bar?"

Jacobe shook his head and motioned for the bartender to come back. "Crown and Coke," he ordered, before turning back to Calvin. "I'm not interested."

A knowing expression covered Calvin's face. "Really. Who's the woman?"

"Who said there's a woman?"

"Whenever a man is uninterested in a beautiful and willing woman it's usually because there's another woman he doesn't want to answer to."

The bartender returned with Jacobe's drink. He took a sip and shook his head. "Not the case here. I'm still single."

"Single and pining, from the looks of it," Calvin said with a grin.

A hand slapped him on the shoulder. Jacobe turned to Isaiah. "Sorry to interrupt, but I think it's time to go."

Jacobe looked at his watch. "We just got here."

"Believe me, it's time to go." Isaiah emphasized the last words.

Calvin straightened. "What's wrong? Is someone giving you any trouble? I can get rid of them."

"Not yet," Isaiah said.

"What do you…" Jacobe's words trailed off. Christy

strolled up behind Isaiah. Her new man, some actor she'd started dating after she'd split with Jacobe's former roommate, best friend and teammate. The real father of her child.

"Hi, Jacobe. Good game tonight," she said in a sweet but hesitant voice. She looked good. Honey-toned skin, curved to perfection, long silky hair. She wore a tight red dress that was high on her thighs and low on the cleavage.

She met his eye boldly. The question that was always in her light brown gaze when they ran into each other still there: *Are we cool now?* Hell, no, they weren't cool. Never would be. Not after what she'd done to him.

He looked to Isaiah. "You know what, it is time to go."

Christy held up her hands. "Don't be that way, Jacobe. There's no reason for you to leave just because I'm here."

He glared at her, too pissed to talk. The way she was so blasé about the entire situation grated on his nerves. Her disregard for the way she'd betrayed him was a slap in his face.

He brushed past Christy without a word. More than ready to get the hell out of there.

"Hey, man, you heard my woman talking to you," the not-quite-B-grade actor she was dating said. "I can't let you disrespect her like that."

Jacobe's rage stiffened his spine and he spun back to the guy. "This ain't your fight, man. Stay out of it."

"It's my fight when you disrespect my woman."

"Your woman doesn't deserve my respect." He cut a glance at Christy.

Christy raised her chin. "It's been four years, Jacobe. Can't we get over it?"

The comment was so stupid he almost laughed and

would have if he wasn't so pissed that she'd asked him that. "Get over it?" He ran a hand across his face and took a deep breath. She wasn't worth the fight. "You know what, you ain't even worth it."

Christy's lip twisted. "You always were emotional and soft. You don't know how to let things go. What happened with Jake wasn't all my fault," she said referring to their…no, her son. "You've got to accept your part."

The word was on the tip of his tongue. The same word that Danielle had used just the other day. He could taste it, feel it with the boiling hot rage searing through his veins. He bit it back. He hated her but wouldn't call her that in public.

"To hell with this, and you."

The actor threw a punch. Jacobe dodged, but the edge of the guy's fist grazed his chin. Jacobe threw a body shot that knocked the wind out of the guy, followed by a swift upper cut that had him sprawled on the floor. He glared down at Christy's date, then at her and shook his hand out.

"But I'm soft," he said with a sneer.

Ignoring the flash of camera phones, Jacobe threw an apologetic look at Calvin, who only shrugged, then turned his back on Christy. Davina stood nearby. He was jittery, jacked up on anger, frustration, need. He could continue to pine for Danielle. Her voice rang through his head: *This was a mistake.*

Or he could move on. He took Davina's hand. Her smile was eager and willing. "Let's go." He led her out of the club.

Danielle stomped across the hall into Debra's office. Debra wasn't there. Grunting, Danielle spun around and marched to the kitchen. Debra was leaning against the counter, sipping from a cup of coffee and reading a trade magazine.

"Did you see that email?" Danielle asked, annoyance in her voice.

Debra slowly lowered the magazine and frowned. "What email?"

"The lead singer for the band we hired to play at the gala next week just found out he has to have surgery. They've got to cancel."

Debra shrugged and went back to scanning the magazine. "Then we'll hire a DJ, instead."

Danielle tapped her foot on the floor. "How are we supposed to find someone on such short notice?"

"I'm not saying finding a replacement will be easy, but it is possible. One of the interns mentioned knowing a DJ. If that doesn't work out, my gynecologist plays drums for a band. He's mentioned giving them a call if we ever need someone to step in."

"Any good band or DJ will be booked already."

"Really? I didn't realize mid-April was prime band season."

Danielle narrowed her eyes, but her foot stopped the incessant tapping. "Don't be annoying."

Debra slapped the magazine on the side of her leg. "You stop freaking out. Is this about that report on Jacobe over the weekend?"

"Why would that report have anything to do with us needing a band for next Friday?"

"The fact that you didn't ask what report means you know what I'm talking about and you are pissed off about it."

More like angry, jealous and confused. "Don't be ridiculous."

"What's ridiculous is you acting like you don't care about what happened with Jacobe over the weekend when you two are dating."

Danielle held up a finger. "We are not dating."

"That long disappearance on the boat the other day says you are."

Heavy footsteps stopped at the door behind Danielle. "That long disappearance was a mistake. At least, that's what Danielle says." Jacobe's deep voice.

Danielle sucked in a breath and spun around. A few days' worth of beard covered his square jaw. Black Nike training pants and a matching shirt made her very aware of every muscled inch of him.

He looked directly at Danielle. "Can we talk?"

She nodded. "Sure. I need to speak to you, too." Throwing a glance at Debra, Danielle ignored her friend's *told you so* look. She led Jacobe toward her office.

"Actually, can we talk outside?"

"Sure." The suggestion was appreciated. She didn't want to be cramped in a room with him when he looked sexy, smelled divine, and memories of the way he'd brought her pleasure in the cabin of his yacht floated through her head.

Danielle traded her heels for a pair of sneakers she kept in the mudroom, and then they walked toward the beach. Lots of clouds blocked the sun. The air was still warm, but when a breeze blew over them Danielle pulled her cardigan tight and crossed her arms.

"What did you want to talk to me about?" he asked.

"I wasn't sure if you still wanted to come to our gala next Friday. I didn't want to put your name on the re-minder emails if the plans had changed."

"Why do you sound like you've changed your mind?"

"I wasn't sure what the thought process was after your fight this weekend."

She wanted to ask about the woman he'd been photographed with leaving the New York club, but didn't. They weren't together. No matter how much jealousy carved away at her insides, who he slept with shouldn't play into his work with the River Watchers. Even if it did play with her personal emotions.

He stopped walking and turned toward her, his face a mask of hard stone. "My thought process? Look, Danielle, if you have something to say, then say it."

"I thought you were changing your image."

"Christy was there. Her new guy threw a punch at me. I'm not going to let a guy try to hit me and just ignore it."

"She was there?"

"Yeah." He ran his hand over his face. "We run into each other every so often. Each time we do she tries to act like we're friends. Like I should be over what happened."

"You're not over it."

"Four years have passed since I found out. I know he's not my son. I get that. But the betrayal—no, the pain of what she did… That is harder to let go. I never really realized how much I liked having a kid until he was taken away from me."

His voice was hollow, hurt. Danielle rested her hand on his tense arm. He covered hers with his. She didn't know what to say, knew he hated bringing this situation up, but she knew he needed to get this out.

"He was nine months old when we found out he had hemophilia. We knew we'd have to be careful as he got older. Watch out to make sure he didn't hurt himself. He kept getting strep throat. Finally, the doctor recommended removing his tonsils before he got much older. They wanted blood on hand, ya know. Just in case things got iffy during surgery because of his hemophilia." A raw, pained laugh. "Christy didn't even bat an eye when the doctors brought up testing me to see if I was a match. She wasn't too surprised when the results came back either. She'd been cheating on me for years."

Pain shot through Danielle's heart. She couldn't imagine the pain, the betrayal he'd felt. "You had no idea?"

"Not really. We argued more as we got older, but I never suspected she'd step out on me. Mostly because I wouldn't step out on her. She'd been there for me for years. When we had Jake, I knew I wouldn't leave her and break up my family the way my dad broke ours. I thought I could trust Christy."

That was the first time he'd brought up his dad around her. She ignored her curiosity about this family and focused on the current conversation. "Do you know who Jake's father is?" she asked quietly.

"Martin is the father."

Danielle sucked in a breath. His roommate? The guy who'd been drafted onto the same team with Jacobe the next year. His best friend. "Martin?"

She remembered the reports of the locker-room fights and disagreements before Jacobe was traded. "That's why you two started fighting so much."

"That's why I was traded." Dark eyes met hers. "I've learned the hard way to be careful about the people I let into my inner circle. I know I can't allow him or old teammates get to me on the court. I try very hard to ignore Christy when I see her. But I *will not* let one of the guys she's sleeping with try to take their insecurities out on me. If they start a fight, I'm ending it."

"I wouldn't expect you not to."

His brows shot up. "I didn't expect you to say that."

"Everyone has the right to defend themselves. If that's what really happened and how things went down, then I'm sorry for what I implied." She lowered her eyes and readjusted the glasses. That explained one thing. "Were you able to calm down after you left the club?"

He lifted her chin so their eyes could meet. "I left with her, but nothing happened."

She pulled away from his touch. "You don't owe me an explanation."

"No, I don't," he said bluntly. When she would have turned away, he stopped her with a hand on her arm. "But I'm giving it to you anyway. Nothing happened because she isn't the woman I'm thinking about when I lie in bed at night. She isn't the woman I want."

The look in his eye said very clearly she was that woman. She bit her lower lip to keep from grinning. That still wasn't a declaration he wanted them to date, but it didn't stop the happiness welling in her chest. She wanted him, too.

"Now that you know the truth about what happened in New York, do you still want me to come? Even though other people besides Debra may think we're together?"

"Of course I want you to come. I'm not worried about what people think. We both know we're just friends, right?"

"Keep saying that." His smile said they were much more. Jacobe turned to stroll down the beach.

Danielle watched him for a few seconds before following, confused and a little thrilled by his response. Maybe if she gave in to this, they could turn into something.

Chapter 9

The crowd filling the country club for the River Watchers silent auction surprised Jacobe. Women in cocktail dresses and men in suits mingled around tables covered with the various items for sale while soft music played in the background. He didn't plan on buying anything. His attendance at the cleanup and the public hearing had already brought attention to the Clear Water permit and had put his name in a good light for wanting to protect the creek and river. Being here tonight should add to that positive chatter. The thought of seeing Danielle increased his interest in attending.

"Jacobe, you made it," Debra said when she checked his name at the door.

The blue dress she wore matched new blue highlights on the tips of her dark hair.

"I promised I'd be here." He looked over her shoulder. "You've got a big crowd."

"Thanks to you. The last blast we sent out that mentioned you would be making an appearance upped the number of ticket sales."

"I'm glad my name could help."

"I appreciate you offering to lend your star power to our cause. Danielle is, too, even though she won't gush over it the way I will. If we hadn't reached our goal in ticket sales, there was a real possibility we all would have been out of a job."

Debra turned and asked one of the people checking names to handle things for a second and escorted him into the main room.

Jacobe followed her and asked. "What do you mean about your jobs being on the line?"

"Danielle's done a great job increasing our revenue, but fund-raising isn't her favorite thing. She'd rather be in the trenches. Some people on the board know that and they made bringing in more donations a big goal for this year."

He had a good idea the person on the board was Liberty. He'd make a donation to the River Watchers tonight.

"Danielle never mentioned her job being on the line depending on the success of this."

"That's Danielle. She connected to the community here. To her, the work is about making a difference not about raising the funds. If she were worried, she wouldn't let us know."

Jacobe glanced around the room. "Speaking of Danielle..."

Debra grinned. "I knew you were waiting to ask about her."

"That obvious?"

"That, plus your eyes are scanning the room. Don't worry, she likes you, too."

"We're just friends." Though he was beginning to think he was breaking through that label and they'd soon be lovers.

"You two can save that lie for someone else. I warned her against getting involved if she thought she'd get attached. Danielle loves a challenge."

"I'm a challenge?"

"Every guy is some type of challenge. You're the hardest type to resist. A sexy basketball superstar with a love-'em-and-leave-'em dating history. She'll get close to you and fall hard. So, don't push for more unless, you know, you really want more. Don't start something knowing one day you'll walk away from her. She's been through that once."

"I didn't leave her. I declared for the draft," he said quickly. Immediately thinking Debra referred to him leaving Danielle in college.

"I'm not talking about you." Interest sparked in her eyes. "Why would you think I was?"

Someone walked over to speak to Debra before he could ask for more of an explanation. Greeting that person led to an introduction to Jacobe, which then opened the floodgates for the people at the auction. He spent what felt like a millennium shaking hands, smiling and taking selfies. Claiming a dry throat and the need for a drink allowed him to break away from the crowd and make his way toward one of the bars set up in the back of the room.

The entire time he'd been greeted he hadn't seen Danielle once. She had to know he was there—his arrival had made too much of a show for her not to. Did that mean she was avoiding him? Debra's words rushed back into his head. Don't start something knowing he'll walk away.

He hadn't exactly walked away from her. They'd known that night was spontaneous, and, yeah, he had meant to call her, but the mistake that was Christy and his good intentions had stepped in the way. Plus, she hadn't seemed hurt by that. Not that she'd show it if she were. Based on what he knew of Danielle, he doubted she'd spent the last few years pining for him based on a one-night stand.

If not him, then who else? She mentioned her parents always having more important things to do than show up for her events. Had they skipped out on this? There was also the boyfriend she'd mentioned but hadn't gone into detail about. She didn't seem angry when she spoke of him, but again, she wasn't the bitter type. Had another guy walked out on her before?

He ordered a Crown and Coke, tipped the bartender, then turned to face the room. He gave tight smiles to the few people who glanced at him with eager expressions, which meant the tide of happy fans was about to descend upon him again. Jacobe sucked in a deep breath to prepare himself. The air stuck in his lungs.

Danielle entered through the double doors that led out to the terrace with Mason and India. She wore a simple black dress that stopped above the knee and cut straight across her luscious breasts. A short-sleeved black cardigan with some type of sparkly stuff along the neckline covered her upper arms, and high heels brought out the curve of her sleek legs. Her hair was pulled back into a smooth ponytail. The glasses were missing. With her back straight and her shoulders back, she surveyed the room both critically and with pride while her companions talked. Just like a general examining the battlefield.

Damn, she was sexy. Prim, proper and perfect. Warmth and anticipation slowly spread through his midsection and then the rest of his body. Maybe he was a challenge she didn't want to deal with. He was also pretty sure he wouldn't be able to give her everything she wanted or deserved: marriage, a house and kids. But at that moment, he knew that he wanted her and every other man in the room to know that she was his.

His feet were moving before he realized what he was doing. Her head turned, and their gazes collided. She didn't look surprised to see him, which meant she knew about his arrival. Knew and still avoided coming to him.

"I heard you were here," she said when he reached her side. "What do you think?"

"Great crowd." He glanced at the man and woman. "Mason and India, right?"

Mason held out his hand. "That's right. Good to see you again, Jacobe. Great job in the game last week."

Jacobe shook his hand. "Thank you. It feels great to be back on the court."

India shook his hand also. "We were just telling Danielle she's putting the rest of us river rats to shame with this gala."

Jacobe glanced between them confused. "River rats?"

Danielle soft laughter washed over him. "It's what we call our little group after a reporter used the term to describe us. He said we 'scurry around the river looking for problems' like rats. Well, we kinda do. Except when we find them, we fix them." Danielle finished with a snap of her fingers that made India and Mason laugh and agree.

"Although with the success of this gala," Mason said,

sliding closer to Danielle until their shoulders touched, "we may have to find a better nickname for you."

Jacobe's stomach tightened when Mason touched Danielle. There didn't seem to be anything sexual, or romantic between the two. That didn't make seeing another man in close contact with Danielle any easier.

"No way," Danielle said, waving a hand dismissively. "I still prefer scrambling in the river to putting on galas." She glanced at Jacobe. "Besides, our newest volunteer is one of the reasons for this success."

Her eyes softened with appreciation and he wanted nothing more than to kiss her. "How is the auction going?" he asked instead.

Danielle glanced at her watch. "It doesn't close until nine. I was just about to walk around and check out the bids. Want to walk with me?"

He wanted to take her out of there and peel that sparkly cardigan and dress off her body. Instead, he held out his arm. "I'd love to."

She hesitated and reached for her glasses, which weren't there, then dropped her hand. "Okay, sure. I'll catch up with you guys later."

She slipped her arm through his. Jacobe have a quick hand wave and led Danielle away. Even with the heels, she was small next to him that her head barely reached his shoulders. He wouldn't have to bend as far to kiss her. He glanced at her lips, shiny with a red lip gloss that made him want to nibble on them like ripe cherries.

They strolled toward the first table. Many people stopped to talk to her and be introduced to him. Their trip around the room took longer because of that.

"Are your parents here?" he asked when they left a group of people to head toward another table. To his pleasant surprise, she hadn't pulled her arm away from his while they walked and talked.

Her hand squeezed his arm and her body stiffened. "No, they couldn't make it."

"I'm sorry."

"It's no big deal. Their work is important."

"So is yours."

She glanced up at him and smiled. "Thank you." She took a deep breath and the tension left her body. "I didn't grow up here, but this is where I ended up after college. I got involved with the community, kayaked the creeks and streams as part of my work, made friendships with the other river rats, and fell in love with the place. I finally feel like I belong somewhere. What I do seems like an uphill battle sometimes, but I love doing it. I make a difference, right here where I live. That is important."

His admiration for her grew even more. Danielle didn't fight for causes just because, she fought because she was connected to them. He hadn't felt connected to anything in a while. Sure, he enjoyed playing for the Gators and believed they'd make the play-offs, but he was ultimately trying to do that to snag a chance at moving to Phoenix. Even that wasn't because he was connected. He hadn't felt like he was a part of something great since his dad died. The feeling compounded when he'd discovered Jake wasn't his.

She stopped to check the items on another table that mostly held jewelry. Her hands lingered over one of the sheets for a simple, sapphire teardrop necklace. Her lips quirked up in a small smile when she looked at it.

"Are you bidding on that?" he asked.

Danielle pulled her hand back. "No. I don't bid on the items here. I leave that for the guests."

"But you like that?"

"It looks like a water drop. I work with water." She stepped back and slid her arm through his again. "Come on, let's go talk to the board members about Clear Water."

They did, and Jacobe did his part to promote the importance of stopping the Clear Water permit.

"Liberty, I know that as a River Watchers board member you care about stopping the permit," Jacobe said. "I hope you take the importance of doing so back to you fellow council members."

Liberty's surprised gaze darted from him to the other people standing around their group. "Of course, but we also have to consider the needs of industry."

"Along with the health and safety of the many kids who play in that creek. That's more important, don't you think." He didn't smile or try to be charming.

Liberty nodded. "Of course."

Danielle's eyes widened and she stared at him after his comments. He had researched the issue. He didn't like of the permit getting issued.

"You're against the permit now?" she leaned in and whispered when the group turned to welcome another person into the conversation.

"Not when it puts at risk the health of those kids I met at the clean up," he replied.

Danielle was pulled away a few minutes later. Jacobe took that as his time to leave the group, but he continued to mingle, sign autographs, take pictures and make his stand on Clear Water known. When asked why he was there he mentioned that he lived on the river and wanted to support its protection. The statements weren't just about improving his image. Somewhere along the way he had started to care.

He decided to bid on a few items. He didn't care much if he won, but hoped that by bidding he'd encourage others to spend more. He didn't get to be alone with Danielle again, and when nine o'clock came she and Debra closed the bidding and went through the bid sheets the interns had gathered up.

He actually won a few things—a new pair of designer sunglasses and a kayak, which meant he'd have to learn to kayak. The only thing he'd really wanted to win—and made sure he had the highest bid on—was one of the last things they announced.

When Danielle and Debra saw the final bid, their eyes widened. Both of their heads jerked up and they looked his way.

"You can't be serious," Danielle said into the microphone.

He shrugged and grinned. The people in the room looked between the two of them.

Danielle shifted and cleared her throat. "The sapphire necklace goes to Jacobe Jenkins."

He winked and raised his glass to her. Debra gave him a look that said she hoped he knew what he was doing. He did—what he didn't know was if he should have.

The party broke up soon after. He pulled out his checkbook to settle for his items.

"Congratulations on your wins," Danielle said.

Jacobe slipped the sunglass case into his pocket and eyed the kayak. "I don't know if that'll fit in my car." He was a tall guy, but he liked his luxury sports sedan.

She chuckled. "No, I doubt it will."

He looked at her. "You've got those boat racks on the top of your Jeep. If I strap it on, can I follow you home?"

"I'll be here a lot longer. We've got to break down and everything."

His disappointment was short-lived when the next thought hit him. "I can wait. I've got a game tomorrow. How about I swing by your place to pick it up before or after the game?"

A beat of hesitation. "Sure." She eyed the necklace box. "What are you doing with the necklace?"

"I'm giving it to the woman in my life."

Danielle frowned. "I didn't know you had a girl-friend."

He leaned in to whisper in her ear. "We've gone on a date, I've entertained your friends, and I've made you come. I'd like to think that makes you the woman in my life."

He saw the spark of desire light up her eyes before uncertainty dimmed them. "Jacobe, I meant what I said. We haven't talked about any of this."

"There's nothing to talk about. We both want this. That's all that matters." Debra and a few other people were heading in their direction. "I'll come by tomorrow." It wasn't a question. He ran his finger across her cheek. Her small smile and quick head nod sent fireworks through his chest. Just the boost he needed before leaving.

Danielle cleaned, grocery shopped, washed clothes and even planted roses on the side of her house, and still she wasn't able to lessen the hum of expectancy strumming through her body as she waited for Jacobe to pick up the kayak.

We both want this. That's all that matters.

Those words had trailed her all day. She did want him. Was nearly convinced being with him wouldn't be so bad. He was doing great with the Gators. If they made the play-offs, she doubted the team would let him go, despite the suspension. That meant he'd be around for a while. No leaving her behind for an opportunity elsewhere. She wouldn't let herself think this was the start of the rest of their lives together, but she also wasn't ready to completely deny the possibility of some type of relationship with him.

Eventually she gave up trying to distract herself and watched the Gators game. The game went into overtime and didn't end until after ten. The Gators won. Considering the postgame interviews, and the team possibly going out to celebrate the win, she didn't expect Jacobe to be able to leave the place until nearly midnight.

The expectation rushed out of her in a disappointing huff. He'd just won a game that pushed them closer to the play-offs. Of course, he wasn't coming to her house for a kayak.

Her body was still tense from a day of anxiously waiting. There was no way she'd get to sleep like this. If she didn't relax she'd be pacing the house. Or, worse, texting Jacobe like a stalker to see if he was still coming by.

Fifteen minutes later she had a bubble bath prepared, candles lit around the bathroom, a glass of wine and a book. She connected her cell phone to the Bluetooth speaker she'd mounted in a corner, and soon the soft sounds of piano music played in the background.

A long, appreciative sigh escaped her when she finally slipped down into the warm sudsy water. After a few minutes, the edginess in her ebbed and she was thoroughly engrossed in the book. Then, even though the story was great, her mind began to wander as it had with every other activity she'd tried to distract herself with that day. Thoughts of Jacobe slipped over her mind just as warm and silky as her bubble bath. The thoughts poured into every nook and cranny of her brain, filling her head with the memories of the way he'd kissed her, the hardness of his erection rubbing against her, the sudden, unexpected pleasure that had exploded through her body when she'd climaxed. The heat of embarrassment she'd felt that day was replaced with the intense fire of need to experience the sensation again.

The chime of her text message alerts interrupted the music. *Jacobe?* Danielle shot up in the tub. Sudsy water splashed over the side. She tossed the book to the floor, hoped it didn't land in a puddle and snatched her phone resting on the window ledge above her tub.

I'm outside. R u up?

"What the…" she stuttered. "He's outside? Now?"

Danielle jumped out of the tub. Water splashed everywhere. The cover of her book was doused and she cringed. Better a paperback than her e-reader. Her fingers flew over the screen with a quick response.

Yes. Give me a sec.

She hurried out of the bathroom and grabbed a T-shirt and a pair of pajama pants from her drawer and slipped them on. She slid on her glasses as she hurried to the front door. Her heart pounded. All the tension she'd tried to relax away in the bath returned in full force.

She gave a quick look through the peephole. Jacobe stood on the other side, looking tall, sexy and way too tempting.

She swung open the door. "Hey, um, the kayak is in the garage. I'll let the door up and you can pull it out."

"You aren't going to invite me in?"

He had no idea how badly she wanted to invite him in. "It's late, and I was in the tub."

His dark gaze swept over her body, then heated. "I see."

A breeze swept through the door, and the wet material of her T-shirt and pants cooled against her skin. Danielle's nipples crystalized to hard tips. Jacobe's eyes lowered, and his tongue did a quick sweep of his lower lip. Danielle glanced down, then bit back a groan. In her haste, she'd grabbed an old white T-shirt. Combined with her wet, mad dash from the tub, the thin material could have clung better only if she were in a wet T-shirt contest. The thin pants of her pink pajama bottoms were no better, sticking to her legs and somewhat transparent in the light from her porch.

He jerked his eyes away, twisted his head to the side and tugged on the waistband of his Gators training pants. Of course her eyes dropped to his crotch. He wasn't rock hard, but he was definitely not flaccid. She pulled her lower lip between her teeth.

"You've got to stop staring at me like that," Jacobe said in a thick voice.

Danielle's gaze snapped up to his. "Like what?"

"Like you want me to peel those wet clothes off your body, carry you to the bedroom and finish what we started on the boat."

She did. "I do." *Oh, hell, I said that out loud.*

He took a step forward and braced his hands on either side of her door. "Don't play with me, Danielle. If I come in this house I'm going to do just that. No long conversations about you being the woman in my life."

"Will I be the only woman in your life?"

He leaned in. "You already are. Now tell me I'm the man in yours."

Her brain wanted to analyze the words. Dig down to find out the meaning. Discover if this meant a relationship or just friends with benefits. Her body and the seductive invitation in Jacobe's eyes made the decision. "You are."

Chapter 10

Danielle's simple declaration filled Jacobe with more excitement than any game win ever had. His hands were on her waist, and a second later he lifted her off her feet. He pressed her soft body into his and covered her mouth in a hot, impatient kiss.

"Bedroom?"

"Down the hall, last door on your right."

He kicked the door closed and took a step forward.

Danielle tapped him on the shoulder. "Lock the door."

He chuckled. "Always practical." He teased, but did lock the door, holding her up and against his body with one arm.

The practical business of keeping out intruders handled, Jacobe carried her quickly down the hall and into her bedroom. Her bedside lamps were on and the glow of candles from the open door of her connected bathroom cast a soft light in the room. Jacobe glanced toward the bathroom.

"Your tub is too small for me, but I will have to get you in my bathtub one day."

A sweet, feminine moan accompanied a slight shiver across her body. He gently set her back on her feet, then slowly unwrapped every inch of her silky skin from the wet T-shirt and pajamas. Back in college, their night together had been rushed. Though he remembered every exquisite detail from then, tonight he wanted to savor his time with her. Starting by taking in how absolutely beautiful her naked body was.

She reached for her glasses and slowly pulled them off. Then she pulled her hair from the haphazard knot at the back of her head. He ran his hands through the thick strands. Bracing her head between his palms, he slowly pulled her forward and lowered his head to kiss her. The tips of her breasts brushed his chest as she rose onto her toes to kiss him. Jacobe lifted her up. Only breaking the kiss when he gently laid her on the bed with her legs still hanging over the side.

He used his legs to nudge her knees apart and stood between her parted thighs. Leaving her body open and on display for his enjoyment. He ran his hands across the soft skin of her thighs. Her muscles danced beneath the tips of his fingers. Her wide dark eyes watched him from beneath heavy lids. The rise and fall of her breasts mesmerized him.

"Can I take my time tonight?"

Her smile was seductive. "Take all the time you want."

Running his hands up her thighs, his thumbs brushed the wet curls between her legs. He wanted to play there. Part her folds and slide his fingers through her delicious warmth. Later. Now was time to savor.

He ran his hands over her round hips, the perfect curve of her sides and the outer swell of her breasts. Danielle's ragged breaths and soft sighs told him she wanted more. He wanted more. Wanted to be buried deep in her silky heat. Leaning over her, but not quite touching her, he ran his fingers from the fluttering pulse in her neck to trace across her parted lips. The tip of her tongue darted out to play with his fingers. The fleeting touch sent shock waves through his body.

Jacobe lowered himself and pressed his lips to hers. He savored her kiss. Tasting her sweetness. Indulging in her soft sighs, sweet moans and the seductive arch of her body against his. He needed to feel her skin on his. He lifted just enough to snatch off his shirt, then kissed her again. The pleasure that burst through him when her skin pressed against his was something he wasn't sure he'd ever get tired of feeling.

His hand completely covered a soft breast. He gently squeezed. Her back arched. He had to taste her.

Danielle's body was on fire. Hotter than the candle flames flickering in her bathroom. Jacobe was the lighter fluid, driving her to lava-like levels. His hands delivered a slow kind of seductive torture as they played over her body. When his tongue slowly ran across the hard tip of her breast she cried out her pleasure.

"Jacobe, yes!"

He tasted her breasts. Teasing, nipping and licking the hard tips. She squirmed beneath him. Her hands clutched his head, holding him in place as her body begged for more. One strong hand ran up her thigh.

"Open for me," he whispered against her breast before drawing her nipple into the welcome warmth of his mouth.

Danielle gasped and her legs flew open. Jacobe ran his finger over the seam that barely hid the swollen bundle of nerves there.

"Are you wet for me?" His lips played against her nipple.

Danielle nodded. "Yes."

"How wet?" His finger made a lazy circle over her clit then dipped to press against the opening of her core. "Almost wet enough."

Danielle would explode if he didn't push into her. Her hands stopped clutching his hair. Pushing one between them, she palmed his cock. "Show me how hard you are."

Jacobe shuddered. His finger pushed into her. Found the sweet spot that sent another wave of need rushing through her.

"That's my general," he said, his lips wrapping around the tip of her breast, his finger pleasuring her with steady strokes.

Danielle's hand slipped past the elastic waistband of his pants. Hot skin over rigid flesh filled her hand.

"No underwear." She didn't want to wait any longer. "Now, Jacobe."

He shook his head. "Not yet."

Strong hands gripped her waist. In a swift movement, he pulled her farther up on the bed. His body lowered until his shoulders could push her thighs apart, and he gave her the most intimate of kisses. The sweet pleasure of the kiss shot through every nerve. She bucked and lifted onto her elbows. His confident gaze held hers as he slowly devoured her.

Her head fell back, the sensations almost too much to handle, definitely too much to feel and watch. Just before she exploded he pulled back.

"No, don't stop," she pleaded.

He dug into the pocket of his pants and pulled out a condom, then pushed them down and kicked them off the side. "Now you're ready."

He quickly covered himself. Slowly he brought the full length of his body over hers. Taking his length in his hand he slowly eased into her, not once breaking eye contact.

Danielle gasped, and her nails dug into the hard muscles of his shoulders. She remembered this. The stretch to accept every thick inch of him. The fullness no one else could match. Except tonight was infinitely better. Then he'd driven her to new heights quickly. Hard and fast and over much too soon. Tonight his strokes were slow. Measured.

"Harder, Jacobe," she begged. "Harder."

He pushed deeper, pulling her legs up so he could fill her more. Her eyes rolled to the back of her head.

"Look at me." The deep command washed over her, leaving no room for argument, and she complied. "Who's in you? Who's making you feel this?"

As if she would ever forget. "You, Jacobe. Oh, my God, you feel so good inside of me."

Her legs tightened around his waist. Her hips lifted to meet each one of his thrusts. He groaned, buried his face in her neck and took her to a place of pleasure she didn't think anyone else would ever carry her to again.

Chapter 11

He didn't stay.

Something about early practice and preparation for the final games before the play-offs. He left her place at two in the morning with a quick kiss and the promise to call her later that day. She understood. A small corner of her mind realized he did have practice and his reasons for leaving were legitimate. The majority of her brain remembered the last time he'd said he would call and she wondered if she was about to be left behind again.

She buried herself in work and even went out to collect samples with the interns instead of sitting in the office doing work that wouldn't keep her mind occupied enough to not think of Jacobe. When Debra asked her out for drinks after work, she said yes and tried not to think about Jacobe not calling. She must have done a decent-enough job of hiding her fears because Debra didn't ask about Jacobe and Danielle didn't bring him up.

When she pulled up to her house after happy hour

and saw Jacobe standing on her porch with his cell phone in his hand, she admitted she was way too happy and relieved to see him.

He looked up and smiled at her when she parked beside his sports car.

"Waiting on me?"

"I was just about to call you."

She had an overwhelming urge to hug him when she walked up to him. Was that something they did now? This was why she didn't do the casual hookup. She hated the freak-out over the boundaries when she'd already seen the guy naked.

Jacobe solved her inner debate by wrapping an arm around her shoulders and pulling her against the heat of his body. Her arms wrapped around his waist, and when he kissed the top of her head she had to suppress a huge grin.

"You're here to get the kayak, right?" she said after she drew back.

"To hell with the kayak." He pulled her back into his arms and kissed her.

She let her worries about him not staying and the questions about what they were to each other rest. She liked their current space.

"You taste fruity," he said against her lips.

"Strawberry daiquiri," she said.

"Hmm." He kissed her again. "Strawberry-flavored Danielle. I like it," he whispered in her ear. His lips tugged at the delicate lobe, then he groaned and pulled back. "I don't like these earrings. They're in my way."

She lifted her hand to the earrings. "Hey, don't insult my jewelry. It's not the earrings' fault you're trying to nibble on my ear on my front porch."

She turned to pull out her keys and unlock the door.

"I'm going to toss out all long, dangly earrings that keep me from doing just that," he said.

She stepped through the threshold. Jacobe wrapped an arm around her waist and pulled her back against him. He kissed her neck. When he touched her ear, she slapped his hand. "No throwing away my earrings."

"What if I keep replacing them with things like this?" he said, motioning with his other hand. She recognized the box that held the necklace he'd bought at the auction.

"You shouldn't have gotten me that."

"You want me to give it to someone else." He pulled his hand back.

Danielle grabbed his wrist. "I said you shouldn't have. That doesn't mean I don't want it." She'd fallen in love with that necklace the second she'd seen it.

"Hold your hair up."

She smiled and pulled her hair off her neck for him to fasten it. When he finished he flicked her earring with his finger. "The blue does kind of match your earrings."

The earrings were made of copper wire with small blue pearls. "They were a gift, too." She turned to face him.

His brows rose. "Who gave them to you?"

"This guy I dated."

She could feel the sudden tension take over his body. "Must have been serious for him to give you jewelry."

"You've already given me jewelry that's much more expensive than these earrings. Are we serious?"

"Was this the college boyfriend? The one you got over me with?"

Her head jerked back. "What? I didn't *get over you* with him. We started dating the year after you left and stayed together until after graduation. I didn't need a rebound after our one-night stand."

"So then it was serious. You two were together for three years."

"That was years ago."

"Then why do you still have the earrings he gave you?"

She touched the earrings. "Because I like them."

"Or because you still care."

"Oh, my God, are you seriously going to be that guy?" She pushed around him and marched into her living area.

His footsteps followed. "What are you talking about?"

She dropped her purse on the couch and spun to glare at him. "Are you going to be jealous because I still have earrings from a guy I dated *years* ago?"

She crossed her arms and raised her chin. They were just earrings, and she didn't even think about her ex when she wore them. Only when people asked her where she got them from did she bring up that they were a gift. His history with Christy was completely screwed up, but that didn't mean she would pay for that woman's mistakes. If they were in this, he'd have to trust her.

What if he never does?

The tension left his body. Not in a quick rush, but what appeared to be a slow and deliberate manner. "No. I'm not that guy."

She nodded, but the tightness of his voice didn't really reinforce the words. Changing the subject to something else was their best bet. "I was going to heat up a frozen meal for dinner, but I can order something, instead. If you planned to stick around. Unless you're too pissed at me now?"

This time when he relaxed it looked natural. He crossed the room, put his hands on her hips and easily lifted her. "I want to kiss you, not argue."

He kissed her, and she wrapped her arms around his neck. All her frustration melted away and the smallest glimmer of optimism filled her again. But when he put her down, his gaze strayed to the earrings again.

Lying in bed naked with Danielle running her fingers across his chest, Jacobe felt he could stay there indefinitely. He'd felt that way a few times hanging with her in college, even when they'd bickered. He'd sometimes think they needed to get past the bull and just admit they wanted each other.

Except he hadn't because he'd been with Christy. He thought about the earrings and the guy who'd given them to her.

He squeezed her shoulder and she tilted her head back to look into his eyes. "Are you still in love with him?"

Her brows drew together and her fingers froze on his chest. "Who?"

"The ex that gave you the earrings."

She sighed and tried to sit up. "Are you still on that?"

He stopped her from leaving his embrace. "It's a fair question."

"What Christy did was reprehensible, but I'm not her."

"I know that. Believe me I do, but I won't get involved with you if you still have feelings for someone else. You two were together for three years. I know it's been a while since you broke up, but I just want to know if anything is still there."

Danielle flipped over until her chest rested on top

of his. He dropped his hand to cup her backside, then tried to focus on the conversation and not how tempting she was.

"We were together a long time. Yes, at the time, we thought we were in love."

"What happened?"

"He was offered an amazing opportunity in another state. We tried for a little bit, but things didn't work out."

"If his opportunity was so amazing, why didn't you go with him?"

Danielle dropped her eyes to his chest. "The original plan was for me to go, but, like I said, it didn't work out."

"He left you behind." Debra's warning stuck in his head.

"I wouldn't view it like that. We wanted different things. Even if he'd asked I doubt we would have made it. Too many demands on his end to expect him to have the time for a relationship."

He didn't need to be in her bed right now, but he was. He should be at home resting for tomorrow's practice. "When you really want to be with someone you find the time to make it work."

She smiled and her eyes sparkled like chocolate diamonds. "I appreciate that. But you have a demanding career, too. You should understand."

"Does he play sports?"

She nodded. "He does."

"Professionally?"

"Yeah." His body stiffened. She must have sensed his thoughts because she shook her head. "Not basketball. He's a football player."

"Who?"

"Does it matter? You two probably don't know each other."

"The world of professional sports is small. I probably do know him. I could guess if I think of the guys who were drafted from our school."

"Luke Kinard," she said.

He did know Luke. He was a friend of Isaiah's and would probably come to a few games if they made the play-offs. Definitely any parties. He wished he hated the guy, but he didn't. It was hard to dislike Luke. He was one of those all-around good guys, and he was very passionate when it came to being eco-friendly. Just the type of guy Danielle would be with.

"He's a nice guy," he said simply.

"He is."

He had a dozen other questions. Questions that would make him sound paranoid. He was done playing paranoid in relationships. Danielle wasn't Christy. He would have to try to trust her.

"Was there anyone else after Christy?" she asked softly.

He snorted and rubbed his forehead. How could he explain to her that he'd thoroughly enjoyed his love-'em-and-leave-'em life after breaking up with Christy without sounding like a pig? He couldn't.

"No."

She was silent for a few seconds. "How did your parents take the situation?"

"My dad died when I was thirteen. Killed by his husband's lover."

Danielle sucked in a breath. "I'm sorry to hear that."

"I thought he was this great guy. He had been great to us. That's one of the reasons I never cheated on Christy. I saw firsthand the trouble that could come from cheating." He ran a hand over his face. Danielle was quiet while he let the hurt and anger from that time die down before speaking again. "My mom took what Christy did hard. When I had Jake she said he was the best thing to come from me. When we found out he wasn't mine, she blamed me for not checking his paternity sooner. We don't talk much. The only other person who would have cared about how I felt was my granddad, but he'd died the year before. I really wished he would have been there then."

"Why?"

"After my dad died, my granddad would take me bowling every Wednesday night. After a couple of sodas, a basket of cheese fries, and a game or two he'd ask me how I was doing, say I could always come to him, but never pushed me to talk. He knew I was spiraling. Those bowling nights reminded me I had someone who cared. My mom was so angry after my dad was killed, she couldn't deal with me. I couldn't understand her anger until after Christy cheated."

Though he never would have taken his anger out on Jake. He wouldn't let any kid of his think they were a burden. If he ever had kids again.

He glanced at Danielle. The empathy in her eyes was more comforting than any words she could speak. There was nothing anyone could say that would make what happened in his past any easier. Talking to Danielle about it was easier than he'd imagined.

Her small hand rested on his chest right over his heart. "You're the man in my life now. If a part of me wanted anyone else I wouldn't have let you in last night. I promise you my fidelity while we're together. If you promise me the same."

He ran the back of his hand across her cheek. "You've

already got that. I've turned down every woman that's approached me here and on the road since reconnecting with you."

Her brow rose and her lip twisted. "Is that supposed to make me feel better?"

"Actually, it is. I haven't found a woman that I wanted to trust enough to be monogamous with. I'm willing to do that while we're together."

The twist to her lips softened to a small smile. He pulled her up by her waist until her body was completely on top of his. "Now kiss me before I have to get up and go."

"You're not staying the night?"

He was tempted, but even if he didn't have practice tomorrow, he wasn't ready to jump into a relationship with overnight stays. "Practice early."

Her smile wavered. He flipped her over onto her back. She giggled, the second of sadness erased from her face. Her laugh and smile made his stomach tighten. He hoped he was right to trust her. He liked her too much to handle being lied to again, which meant he couldn't let Danielle know how much of his heart she already had in her hands.

Chapter 12

Jacobe faked left, and the player guarding him fell for it. Stepping back, he shot the basketball toward the goal from the three-point line. Time slowed to an earthworm crawl as he watched the ball travel. It swooshed through the hoop a millisecond before the game-ending buzzer sounded.

Several seconds passed before the rush of adrenaline and excitement infiltrated his bloodstream. Jacobe jumped up and pumped his fist. His teammates hurried over and the crowd in the stadium went crazy with cheers. With that shot, he'd just secured the Gators' place in the play-offs.

He looked over the heads of the people celebrating around him on the court to the seats behind the bench. Danielle and Debra were both there, jumping up and down and clapping. A month in and he automatically looked for her behind the bench. The high rushing through his system couldn't be topped. They won, were going to the play-offs, and his girl was there watching.

He moved with the wave to the side of the court. More hugs and hand slaps with Kevin, Isaiah and the rest of the team. Coach Simpson came over and slapped Jacobe on the back.

"That's how you do it!" Coach screamed.

Jacobe went through the quick interviews with the reporters on the side of the court before going back into the locker room. Champagne popped, and people laughed and talked big about how they were going to go all the way in the play-offs.

"We're here, but that doesn't mean we're guaranteed the championship," Coach Simpson said. "We've built a championship-level team here, let's keep up the momentum and bring that trophy home." He looked at Jacobe. "Then come back next year and do it again."

Brian and a few other owners had come into the locker room. Brian came over and held out his hand to Jacobe, who was too stoked not to take it.

"I didn't think you were committed to the Gators," Brian said. "I didn't think you wanted to be in Jacksonville. But the work you're doing with the River Watchers and how you're leading this team to the play-offs is changing my mind. If you want to come back I won't oppose your re-signing."

"I appreciate that, Brian. We'll worry about next season when we get through the play-offs."

"Fair enough." Brian shook his hand again, then went on to talk to the other members of the team.

Looked like the team owners were over their concerns about his behavior.

He glanced around the locker room at his teammates. Even though the Gators had been able to win during his suspension, when he'd returned to play he'd increased their shot percentage and the point spread of their wins. Between that and the extra press he got for his endeavors to improve the community, he had no doubts they would want him to re-sign next year. The work they'd done to build up the team and win games filled him with pride. He'd always dreamed big. Would always be proud of what they accomplished.

Isaiah, Will and Kevin walked over. They were showered and dressed for the postgame interviews, Isaiah in his signature bow tie, Will in a designer T-shirt and jeans, and Kevin in a tailored suit that allowed his arm and neck tattoos to peek out.

Kevin watched him suspiciously. "What's up with that look?"

Jacobe stood. He too was dressed and ready for the interviews. "What look?"

"The look I haven't seen since the last game of high school or college. The 'I'll miss this' look."

"Nah, man, I don't know what you're talking about." Jacobe hid his guilt behind a grin. Those were where his thoughts were going. A year ago he wouldn't have cared if his teammates knew he was looking to sign elsewhere. A year ago he hadn't cared much about what the guys thought. Now he did, and he didn't want to give them a reason to doubt his commitment before the play-offs.

He'd texted Danielle earlier and asked her to hang around to wait for him. He pulled out his phone to text her again.

Shower done. Now postgame interviews. Can you still stick around?

A few seconds later, his phone chimed.

If you want me to I will.

You know I want you to. I'll make it quick.

☺

The smiley face she sent back made his lips curve upward. That was the other good thing about being in Jacksonville: having Danielle at the games. If he did make that move, what would she say? He'd left her once and she'd understood the reasons. Would she understand this, or would she just compare him to Luke? Both thoughts felt wrong.

The postgame interviews were full of the expected questions: "How do you feel?" and "Congratulations on making that shot." The effort he took to not look at his watch and hurry things along was staggering. He wanted to get out of there with Danielle.

"Jacobe, not only are you conquering the court," one reporter said, "but you're also trying to conquer the environment. Are you turning into a tree hugger?"

Jacobe laughed and shook his head. "I've recently had my eyes opened to a lot of the challenges threatening the river. I live and work here. All I'm trying to do is make the world a better place where I can."

"Does this have anything to do with Danielle Stewart? Are the reports that you two are dating true?"

His relationship with Danielle didn't have a damn thing to do with the results of tonight's game or the play-offs. He didn't comment on his personal life and wouldn't start now. "Danielle and I are cool. I've known and respected her for years. I'm just happy to work with her to protect the river."

Another reporter caught his attention. "You're a free agent next year. After leading the Gators to the play-offs, a lot of teams are going to be interested in you. There are rumors of the creation of a superteam in Phoenix and that you're on the short list of possible recruits. Do you want to confirm or deny?"

His agent must be doing a good job talking him up to Phoenix. From the comments Jacobe had gotten tonight, the word was getting out that he was considering leaving. "Hey, man, I'm just trying to get through this season. I'll worry about what happens in the off-season after we win the championship."

His prediction earned few laughs. Many in the crowd didn't look convinced. Let them wonder. Until he got through this season and thought things out, he wasn't making any hard decisions.

The interviews finally ended and Jacobe hurried out of the pressroom and back to the court, where Danielle would be waiting for him. She didn't like hanging out near the locker room, which he could understand. She also preferred to stay away from the media, which made him more comfortable, especially since the press were starting to ask questions about their relationship. His cell phone rang. One glance at his agent's number and he stopped to take the call.

"Eric, what's up?"

"What's up is that you're the number-one trend on Twitter right now." Eric's voice was excited.

"I don't care about that."

"You should. There are so many people sharing that final shot that I'm afraid the internet will implode, which is good for you and here's why. I just got off the phone with the Phoenix front office."

"I thought we were keeping that quiet. I'm getting asked questions about it. Questions I don't need right now. I'm trying to get to the finals here."

"As you should, but are you telling me you don't want to hear what they have to say?"

He couldn't say that. "What did they say?"

"They want you. Bad. They realize you've got to get through this season, but they've already secured Warren Hackley and Charles Johnson."

"Shit, for real?" Warren and Charles were two of the best players in the league. Combined with himself, the league might as well give them the trophy every year.

"Would I call you with this if I were lying? Listen, they know you can't promise anything yet, but they're already throwing out offers."

"How much?" Eric told him and Jacobe had to cock his head to the side and ask him to repeat. He'd been in the league for years and made his share of millions, but even this was an offer damn near impossible to refuse.

"Now, do you want me to tell them to shove off?"

"No. Tell them I'm interested. If that's their offer and they're willing to wait until this season is over, then we'll talk more. I owe all of my focus to the Gators right now."

"Of course. You're a good man, but also a smart man. I'll let you know if anything changes, okay."

"Okay."

"And good game."

He thanked Eric and ended the call. The remainder of the walk to meet Danielle was a blur. He liked what he had here, but, damn, you didn't just say no to millions of dollars because you liked an area. He'd have to put the offer out of his mind until the play-offs were over. But if they actually won the finals, Phoenix might want him even more, which would only make contract negotiations easier. He was finally getting what he wanted— to be recognized as an elite player on an elite team.

Danielle was sitting in an aisle seat right near the entrance into the stadium. She was scrolling through her phone with one hand and toying with the end of her hair with the other. No cute cardigan, but she was still sexy in her Gators T-shirt and tight jeans. She looked up when he came in. She jumped up from the chair and hurried over. He gripped her waist and hoisted her up for a kiss.

"You played awesome tonight. Congratulations on the game-winning shot."

Her chocolate eyes shining like diamonds behind her glasses, warm delicious curves in his arms and the smile on her face made him never want to let her go. A crazy thought popped into his head. "Would you ever move away with me?"

Her smile changed into a look of confusion. Then she shook her head and grinned. "Stop playing."

"What if I wasn't? What if I wanted to move to Canada tomorrow? Would you go with me?"

"What if I wanted to move to Mexico tomorrow? Would you go with me?"

No. The answer was immediate. He wanted her in his life, but things were going the way he wanted. If Danielle left and asked him to uproot everything, he wouldn't be able to leave this behind.

"Forget I brought it up." He lowered her back to her feet and took her hand in his. Questions filled her eyes. She looked like she was going to question him more, then shook her head and smiled.

"Let's go celebrate you making it to the play-offs." She squeezed his hand.

"That sounds great."

Danielle rushed from her office to the copy machine. There were no sounds of paper sliding from the machine. She swore silently. The board meeting was less than thirty minutes away and they were supposed to vote on the written comments Danielle had prepared concerning the Clear Water permit to submit to the county. They were similar to the ones she'd submitted to the state, but since Liberty was on council, she needed to make sure there weren't any potential problems. She had made copies for each member to approve—or would have if the machine was working.

Lights flashed and something beeped. She pulled out the paper tray on the front, but it was full. Frowning, she looked at the warning.

Out of toner. Seriously? She checked the shelf next to the machine. The toner shelf was empty. Danielle marched down the hall to the receptionist.

"Do we have any more toner?"

She shook her head. "Sorry, we're out. I just sent one of the interns down to the office-supply store for more."

"Crap. I need to make copies."

"You can try the printer in the interns' office. It might work today."

"*Might* is the important word."

She spun on her heels and marched toward her office. She pressed all the buttons to send the document to the printer in the interns' office.

"What are you frowning about?" Debra asked from the door.

"The printer is out of toner and I'm sending this document to the interns' printer."

"Don't bother," Debra said. "It jammed earlier and there was the faintest of burning smells. That's why I'm here—to get you to sign off on the purchase of a new one."

"Damn! Does anything work around here?"

"Whoa, what's all this?" She came farther into Danielle's office and pushed the door shut. "What gives?"

Danielle let out a long breath and plopped down into the chair behind her desk. "I think I missed a hint or something with Jacobe."

"How?"

Danielle gave Debra a brief rundown of Jacobe's question about her moving away with him and her response.

Debra played with the blue-tipped end of her plait and considered Danielle's story. "Do you think he was serious?"

"I didn't at the time. I listened to the entire postgame interview later. A reporter asked about him going to Phoenix. Jacobe mentioned when we first reconnected about the opportunity to play for a better team. What if that's really in the works? What if he asked me that because he wants me to go to Phoenix with him if he relocates?"

"Is this the same interview where he said you two were *cool*?" Debra made air quotes.

Danielle fought not to flinch. She readjusted her glasses and frowned. "You're right. I'm reading too much into things."

She barely saw Jacobe off the court or out of the bedroom. She had expected his schedule to be busy after his suspension ended and even more so when he made the play-offs. What she hadn't expected was the feeling that she really was in a friends-with-benefits situation instead of a true relationship. He never stayed the night, never asked her to stay with him. She came to the games and cheered for him, but then he told the media that they're *cool*. She was falling in love and he thought they were...cool?

"I think your response was perfect. You're guarding your heart, which is smart with a guy like him. Don't let him think you'll drop everything and follow him if he's not willing to do the same."

"I wouldn't drop everything and move away with him. I don't really expect him to do the same."

"Then what's the problem?"

"I don't know. I think he was hinting around at that, but I'm frustrated he would even consider that when he just told the world that we're *cool*. He's still guarded with me."

"I don't think the issue is if he asked you to move or not. The real issue is how Jacobe feels about you. I like Jacobe a lot, but you've got to look out for yourself first. Don't let him have more of your heart than he deserves."

Debra was right. Danielle had been in this situation before. She'd thought she and Luke were serious, but when he'd gotten the offer to play in Denver he'd taken it. She didn't begrudge him for doing so, but it had stung to discover that he hadn't believed they're relationship would have survived the move. If Jacobe had hinted around at her going to Phoenix, why? Was it because he cared for her? She needed answers to that before making any decision.

Her desk phone rang before she could reply. Debra reached for the door handle. "Think about what I said."

Danielle nodded, but didn't answer. She picked up the phone. "Danielle Stewart, how may I help you?"

"Danielle," her mom said. "Is it true? Are you dating that Jacobe Jenkins?"

Jacobe may have hedged with the media, but she wouldn't with her mom. "Yes, I am."

"Why?" her mom asked. Sounding as disgusted and disbelieving as she would if Danielle had said she didn't give a damn about doing community service. "He's not the right guy for you."

"How do you know that?"

"I'm no sports reporter, but I follow them enough to know he's a troublemaker in the league. Getting in fights and sleeping around with various women. You can't trust a guy like that. Plus, what good does he do in the community? You know he's only interested in the environment because he's trying to butter you up."

"Actually, he gives back a lot." She started to go into the various charities and organizations he donated do, but her mom cut her off.

"Tax write-offs, nothing more. Now, why don't you call up that sweet guy you dated in college? He was a pillar in the community and much better for you."

"Mom, you and Dad haven't come to Jacksonville to see me in over a year. Every time you say you're going to visit, something more important comes up. When I try to get you to pick a good weekend for me to visit, you're doing something else and the timing isn't right. I doubt you know who or what is good for me."

Her mom sputtered. "Danielle, that's not fair. We love you."

"I know you do, but that doesn't mean I'm a priority for you, either. So please don't comment on my personal life." She glanced at the clock. Ten minutes until the board meeting. "I've got to go. I'll call you later. I love you."

She hung up without waiting for an answer. Already

the guilt for talking to her mother that way crept up her throat. She hadn't been disrespectful, not really, but she'd never been so blunt with her mom before. She'd hear more about that later.

Her cell phone dinged with a new email. Danielle rubbed the bridge of her nose and sighed. She should ignore it—the way this day was going any email was probably bad news. It could also be something important.

She stood and grabbed the items she needed for the meeting. She had emailed the comments to the board earlier so they didn't really need hard copies. She picked up her phone and opened the email while walking to the door. She froze right before exiting.

Speak of the devil and the devil will rise, she thought.

An email from Luke. He still did a lot of work in the community and occasionally would toss leads for new donors or projects her way. They had moved on. The romantic feelings from college were gone.

Danielle,

I just finished the details for a trip to Malawi with the Water for Kids Foundation. Me and a few other athletes are going as part of their initiative to install wells and water filters to some of the remote villages. They mentioned having a few environmental activists come along with us. When asked who to invite, I immediately thought of you. I know you've always admired their work.

Trip is in early summer. Late May or early June. Check your calendar.

Luke

PS: I'll send the list of athletes later. I know you want to know who's going.

She scanned the email again, and then a third time. The trip of a lifetime. The Water for Kids Foundation was the same group she'd told Jacobe about that day on the boat. Not only would the trip give her the opportunity to do something she'd always wanted to do, it would probably be highly publicized and would bring greater attention, and donors, to the River Watchers.

Her heart jumped with excitement. But concern made her chew her bottom lip. Leaving the country on a trip with Luke probably wouldn't go over well with Jacobe.

Maybe Jacobe will want to go.

Luke did say athletes were going. There might be room for one more.

Except Jacobe hadn't liked the idea of a service trip when they discussed it that day on his yacht.

The office door swung open. Danielle quickly stepped back to avoid being hit.

"Oops, sorry," Debra said. "We're ready to start. Wait, what's wrong now?"

"I don't have time to say," she said, meeting Debra's eyes, "but believe me we will need to be seated, at a bar, with drinks when I tell you."

Chapter 13

The conversation with Debra was the only thing on Danielle's mind when Jacobe called and asked if she'd like to have dinner at his house that evening. For her own sanity she needed to find out where they stood. She hated to be in this situation. She'd hoped they were on the road to seriously dating until she'd seen the interview.

She parked her Jeep right outside of the garage of his two-story brick home. His house was surrounded by palm trees and lush greenery. She couldn't see the river from the front, but combined with the wooded surroundings, his place was a perfect escape from the bustle of the city.

Jacobe met her at the door wearing a blue gingham shirt and gray chinos. "Right on time."

He took her hand and led her through the house. Soft jazz played in the background and candles were lit throughout the house.

"What's all this for?"

"All what?" He glanced over his shoulder at her with a teasing smile.

On the back terrace overlooking the river, there was a table set with a white tablecloth, candles and silver-covered platters. Jacobe let go of her hand and crossed to a bottle of champagne chilling next to the table.

Danielle crossed her arms and narrowed her eyes. "Okay, what's going on?"

He twisted out the cork in the champagne. "It's all an effort to bribe you."

"Bribe me to do what?"

"Come with me to all the away games during the play-offs and, hopefully, the semi-finals and finals." He poured champagne into two flutes and handed one to Danielle.

Danielle barely kept her jaw from dropping. "What?"

"I want you with me throughout the play-offs. I like having you at the games. I like hearing you cheer for me, and I really like seeing you after all the press stuff is over. I know you have work, and the Clear Water permit stuff going on, but I'm willing to cover the costs of airfare, hotel and whatever Debra needs to let you go with me."

"I'm surprised you want me to go."

Jacobe froze in the middle of taking a sip of the champagne. "Why would you think that?"

"I don't know—maybe because at your press conference you said we were cool. What does that mean?"

"Oh, that." He turned to put the champagne on the table.

Danielle scowled. "Yes, that."

"I don't talk about my personal life with the media. They already knew the answer, so asking was just to try and get more out of me. If I'd said anything else about us then it's a new headline. There's a new woman in Jacobe Jenkins's life. Now everyone wants to know about you. The paparazzi come out, the bloggers start tearing you apart, and people start digging into your personal life."

She slowly walked over to him at the table. "I guess I can understand that, but did you start to think about how that would sound to me?"

"No," he said as if it were obvious that he wouldn't. "You know where we stand."

"Actually, I don't."

He took her hands in his and stared her in the eye. "I trust you, Danielle. More than I've trusted another woman in years. When you first mentioned wanting a relationship, my first thought was to step back and leave you alone. That's what I've done for years. Except, I couldn't."

So much anticipation swelled up inside of her, and it mingled with a bit of hope that the declaration meant what she wanted it to. That his feelings were just as strong as hers. "Why?"

"Because I walked away from you years ago. I wasn't going to do that again."

Her heart beat so hard against her ribs she wondered if it would bruise. She took a step closer to Jacobe. The swell of emotions filling her threatened to explode like a shaken bottle of champagne.

"Jacobe, I—"

"Shhh," he cut her off with a kiss.

Thank God he had. They were way too early in their relationship for her to blurt out what she was about to say. She was scared that the words had nearly bubbled out of her mouth without forethought simply because he wanted her with him during the play-offs. He pulled back just enough to trace soft kisses across her lips, over her chin and back.

Danielle accepted the distraction. She wrapped her arms around his neck and pressed her body against the hard heat of his. Her breasts grew heavy and languid heat took over her bloodstream.

"You keep kissing me like this," Jacobe said, between kisses, "and I'm going to forget about dinner."

Danielle rose higher on her toes and pulled his lower lip between her teeth. "You kissed me first."

Jacobe lifted his head. "Are you very hungry right now?"

Danielle shook her head. "I'm far from starving."

He swept her up into his arms. "Good."

He quickly took her back through the house and ultimately to his master bathroom. Candles were lit in there already. He set her on her feet, then moved away to turn on the water in his tub.

"You want to take a bath?"

"I want to make love to you in the tub. This was for after dinner." He picked up a jar of oil and poured some into the rising water. "I've thought about you in the tub ever since that first night at your house." Next he opened bubble bath and put a generous amount into the water.

Danielle's body heated as she watched him. "The food will get cold."

He pulled off his shirt and tossed it to the side on the floor. Her breath caught in her chest and her gaze slid over every wonderful inch of his chiseled perfection. "Then let's eat."

He moved to walk past her to the door. Danielle hooked her fingers in the belt loop of his pants and pulled him back to her.

"That's what I thought." His smile was cocky before

he lifted her up for a kiss. Jacobe carried her over to his enormous tub.

He undressed her slowly. His warm lips and wicked tongue flicked over every inch of skin he revealed as he pulled off her cardigan, T-shirt, and knee-length skirt. By the time he removed her underwear, her hands were clutching his shoulders, her breaths shorts pants and her body nearly boneless with desire.

Jacobe held her in his arms again then lowered her into the tub. The tub was so large that the water barely covered her waist.

"It's not ready yet," she said.

He eased her backward until she rested against the warm ceramic of the tub. "Shh, just relax."

He reached for a thick washcloth. After dipping it into the water, he picked up the soaking cloth and let the warm drops trickle over her body. Jacobe repeated the movement, his eyes dark and intense in the candle-light as he teased her. The warm rivulets flowed over her in slow, erotic streams.

"Let me take care of you," he said in a low, seductive voice.

He used the cloth to gather the suds from the rising waters and grazed the soft material across her parted thighs, up her stomach and around her breasts. He bathed her with slow precision, each stroke increasing her desire. Her head fell back and her legs spread wide. His fingers replaced the cloth, tracing down her neck and chest, swirling around the hard tip of her breast and the sensitive skin of her midsection.

His hand brushed the curls between her legs. Plea-sure zipped across her skin. Gasping, Danielle's eyes opened to slits and she watched him. The smile on his face was all masculine pride. He gently ran his fingers across her core. Teasing and tormenting her. Danielle's hands gripped the edges of the tub. Her eyes never left his.

One thick finger pushed into her. Her mouth fell open with a silent gasp. His lips curved higher. With deliberateness, he drove her to the brink, holding her captive with his intense gaze. With each wondrous slide of his hand in and out, her thoughts fled and all she wanted was more. To have Jacobe touch her like this and never stop. The erotic pressure built. She pulled her lower lip between her teeth. Her body tightened more and more with pleasure. She exploded with a wave of delicious sensation. Her cry echoed around the bathroom. Her vision blurred and her heart beat frantically in her chest.

Jacobe stood slowly and stopped the water. She watched through half-lowered lids as he quickly peeled off his clothes. He slid on a condom then lowered himself into the tub. He took her into his arms and Danielle met his kiss with renewed passion. He flipped their positions until her legs straddled his waist.

Danielle dropped her hands between them, took him into her hands and lowered herself onto his erection. Her body was overly sensitive from his earlier attentions and she moaned in exquisite pleasure with each filling inch. Jacobe took her face in his hands and brought her forward for a kiss, his hips pushing up with each of her downward slides.

He leaned back and stared at her, his gaze possessive. "You're so damn sexy, Danielle." His hands slid over her shoulders and down her arms before resting on her waist. "So sexy and all mine." His hips pushed up hard and deep. "Tell me you're mine."

Danielle gasped and clasped his arms. The pleasure

was so intense she couldn't stop a grin from curving her lips. "Yours, Jacobe. Only yours."

Several minutes later, Danielle lay with her back against his chest in the tub. The water was still warm and silky, and her body felt just as fluid. She could stay there forever. In his arms, forever. Because she loved him.

"Will you come with me during the play-offs?" Jacobe asked.

The excitement that he wanted her with him was still there, but the concern of giving up so much of her life to follow him made her hesitate. He'd already said he wouldn't disrupt his life for her. Was she being unrealistic and foolish to consider doing it for him?

"That's a lot of time away," she answered.

"Which is why I want you to come."

She took a deep breath. "Jacobe, I don't know."

"Forget it," he said, and tried to sit up.

Danielle pushed back so he couldn't get out. "Stop. You can't get mad when I bring up a valid point."

"I'm not mad. I'm surprised you don't want to come."

"I didn't say I don't want to come. I'm telling you that it's a lot of time away from my job. A lot of time at a very important time."

"I get it. You can't leave right now."

She shifted sideways in his tub to meet his eye. "That, and you're asking me to disrupt my life, drop everything and follow you around the country. But you describe us as being *cool*."

"What are you asking, Danielle? What do you want me to say?"

She wanted him to say he loved her. That he wanted her there not just as a lover but as part of his emotional support. Someone that he could lean on if they lost and who would celebrate any victory with the same enthusiasm and pride he would feel. But Jacobe wasn't likely to lay out any of those emotions at her feet. Those were the wishes of a woman who wanted to be more to him than she probably was.

"Do you want a cheering section, or me?"

"You, Danielle." His dark eyes were filled with an intensity that made her heart flutter. An intensity that promised her that one day he would say those words. "Only you. I haven't had a woman in my life for years. Seeing you the night we made the play-offs. That did something to me."

The words were a warm, happy squeeze around her chest. There was little else he could say to make her feel any better.

"I can't make it to all the games, but I will come to as many as I can."

The tension seeped from his body. The arm around her waist tightened. "Cool."

Danielle laughed. "That's all I get? Cool? After all that sulking and pouting."

"Hey, I don't sulk," he said, and kissed her neck. Jacobe ran a hand up her arm and squeezed her shoulder. "Will you stay here tonight?"

It was the first time he'd brought up either of them spending the night. She wasn't going to Malawi. Wasn't even going to worry Jacobe with the idea of her going. She wasn't sure when he'd be comfortable enough to say he loved her, but she felt his feelings for her. They were more than just the feelings a man had for a woman he only considered a lover.

She turned in his arms and straddled his hips. "I'd love to." When she kissed him she did so with every ounce of love flowing through her.

Chapter 14

"Let's hear it for the Eastern Conference Champions!"

A roar of cheers went up from the crowd in the Suite, a downtown club where the Gators were celebrating winning the semifinals. Danielle lifted her hand and cheered with them. Jacobe wrapped an arm around her neck and pulled her in to kiss her cheek. They were at one of the tables in the VIP section. Kevin and Debra were also there. Jacobe had also suggested she invite the rest of the river rats, who were out on the dance floor enjoying the party.

"This party is amazing," Danielle said over the music and cheering.

Jacobe lowered his head to speak directly into her ear. "If we make the finals, then the next party will be even better. The Gators haven't made it to the semifinals in ten years. I'm proud to be a part of it."

He squeezed her closer against his tall, hard body.

The room full of people and the sounds of the music became a distant hum. Danielle snuggled back into him. She could barely hear his moan, but she felt the rumble of it through his body.

"You're making me want to sneak you out of here," he murmured against her ear.

She wanted him to sneak her out of there. In the weeks since he'd asked her to attend the games with him, things had been great. No more leaving in the middle of the night, or pretending like they were just "cool." He still hadn't said anything in the media about their relationship, which she was okay with, but everyone on the team knew she was Jacobe's woman.

"Will you two stop," Debra said, looking between Danielle and Jacobe. "I'd tell you to get a room, but I'm afraid that you'll actually leave me here with this one." She pointed to Kevin.

Kevin laughed and raised his glass to Debra. "You'd love to be alone with me."

"Oh no, my mama taught me why I never should be alone with a guy like you," Debra replied, waving a finger.

Danielle grinned at the exchange. Debra was a fan of Kevin, and he had flirted with her constantly since Danielle started hanging with the group, but Debra had told Danielle she wasn't ready to be the next woman to have Kevin's baby.

"Whatever," Kevin said. His sly gaze slipped to Jacobe. "I guess you'll be paying up pretty soon."

Jacobe's body stiffened. Danielle glanced at him. He shook his head at Kevin. "Not quite there yet."

"What's that about?" Danielle asked.

Jacobe smiled and kissed her forehead. "Nothing. Kevin just jumping to conclusions."

She had a feeling it was more than that but dropped it. Kevin sipped his drink and winked at Danielle. She got the feeling she was missing something.

"Hey, look who just got here," Isaiah interrupted.

Jacobe looked up and his arm around her tightened. She turned to face Isaiah and her stomach dropped.

"Luke?" she said with disbelief. Every time she saw him she was struck by how he seemed to always look like the nice boy next door. Bright smile, friendly gaze and stylish but conservative clothes.

Luke's smile widened. "Danielle, I didn't expect to see you here." He glanced at Jacobe, then back at her. "How are things?"

Jacobe pulled Danielle tighter against him. "Things are great."

Danielle's lips pressed together. She could answer herself and didn't need him to puff up just because Luke was there.

"Things are well. What are you doing here?"

"I'm here to celebrate the Gators' win. Isaiah and I are good friends. I tried to make it into town for the game, but the flight got delayed. I'll be in town up to the finals, then it'll be time for our trip to Malawi. I planned to get in touch with you while I was in town. You know we're really looking forward to having you on board."

Danielle broke into a cold sweat. She'd assumed Luke's plans had changed when he didn't email again. He must have assumed her silence was acquiescence.

Jacobe cleared his throat and shifted next to Danielle. "Going where?"

"Luke is working with Water for Kids on a trip to Malawi to dig wells and provide water filtration for remote villages. They're taking a few environmental activists to provide guidance on protecting the limited water resources. He asked me to go."

"That's great," Jacobe said. "You always wanted to go on a trip like that."

"You want me to go?"

"I remember you said you always wanted to work with them. Well, now's your chance. That's cool." He sounded like he was all for it, except he'd pulled away from her.

"It's settled," Luke said. "Danielle, I'll call you on Monday to talk about the details." He slapped Isaiah on the shoulder. "Come on, let's get a drink."

Isaiah threw an apologetic look at Jacobe. He didn't look at Danielle before he followed Luke.

Jacobe slid out of the booth. "I'm going to get another drink, too."

"I'll join you," Kevin said.

Debra turned wide eyes toward Danielle when they walked away. "You didn't tell him you were going?"

"I wasn't going. I decided not to go the night he asked me to come to the play-off games. I didn't think I needed to tell him about the invitation. How was I supposed to know Luke would out me?"

Debra took a deep breath. "What are you going to do?"

Danielle looked at Jacobe talking to Kevin at the end of the bar. He glanced back at her. She smiled. He turned away. A dull ache started in her chest. "I don't know."

Jacobe sipped from his beer and glanced toward the windows. Moonlight glistened off the river in the distance, but he didn't see it. His mind was focused on Danielle's lie. That she would plan to leave the country with her ex and not mention it to him at all. He saw her reflection in the glass as she walked up behind him.

"Are you mad at me for not mentioning the mission trip?

"I'm curious about why you kept the trip a secret."

In the reflection, he noticed her lips pressed together. She looked uneasy, which made him uncomfortable. Had he finally trusted a woman only to be fooled again?

"I wasn't keeping it a secret. I forgot to mention that he made the offer."

"That's a convenient excuse."

"It's not a convenient excuse. It's what happened. Luke emailed me weeks ago about the trip. I wasn't sure if I was going, but the night you asked me to come to the play-off games I knew I wasn't going."

He turned to face her. "You were considering it?"

"I was. I've always wanted to do something like this. Of course, I would consider going."

"You'd go out of the country with your ex-boyfriend even though you're dating me?"

"It's a working trip. It's not like I would be going on a vacation with Luke. There's nothing wrong with it."

"Well, it doesn't matter now. Because you're not going."

Her brows drew together. "Are you forbidding me?"

"You said yourself you weren't going, so that's the end of it."

He tried to walk past her. She grabbed his arm to stop him. Her eyes flashed with an anger so sharp he wouldn't have been surprised if her glasses shattered. "If I hadn't decided not to go, are you saying you would have told me not to go?"

He ran a hand over his face. Frustration crawled over every inch of his skin. "I shouldn't have to tell you not to go. You should know better than to take a trip out of the country with your ex-boyfriend."

As soon as the words left his mouth and he saw fury on her face, he knew he'd made a mistake.

"I should have known better?"

He reached for her hand. "Danielle, listen—"

She snatched her hand away and took a step back. "I should have *known* better. Even if I chose to go, that doesn't mean anything about our relationship. You said you trusted me."

"I trust you. I don't trust him."

"What's that supposed to mean?"

"No guy asks his ex to take any type of trip with him unless he has other intentions." He meant that with everything in him. "I saw the way Luke looked at you. The way he looked at us together. He didn't like it and he wants you back."

She threw up a hand and turned away. "Now you're being ridiculous. Luke and I are just friends."

"You can't be friends with an ex."

"Just because you hate Christy doesn't mean everyone who breaks up hates each other." She sucked in a breath and her mouth snapped shut.

Anger, frustration and jealousy seethed through every poor of his body. When she took a step toward him he moved backward.

"I'm sorry," Danielle said. "I should have brought her up."

"Don't be. You said what you meant. I meant what I said earlier. You shouldn't have even considered going out of town with him."

"I wanted you to come with me," she said. "Several athletes are going. That's why Luke is going. I would have asked you to come."

"When is this trip?"

"Early June."

"That's during the finals. Right after I'll be preparing to go to Phoenix."

Her eyes widened. "You are going to Phoenix?"

"The offer they made is hard to refuse." He shrugged. "I'm not sure what I'm going to do. If I go to Phoenix we'll be the team to beat. My chances of winning a championship not just next year but for several years go up. It's the chance of a lifetime."

"When were you going to tell me about Phoenix?"

"After the play-offs." When he was also going to ask her to go with him.

"So it was over when the play-offs ended. You asked me to support you only so you could leave the second you got what you wanted."

The words to deny her accusations sat heavily in his throat. He wanted to tell her the truth, that he wanted her with him wherever he went, that he was falling in love with her. But he wouldn't put his feelings out there when she was considering leaving. He wasn't going to start checking up on Danielle. He wasn't going to worry about her sleeping around or going back to her ex. He'd been in one of those paranoid situations before. If Luke was who she ultimately wanted, then she could have him. If she wanted to go to Malawi with him, let her go.

"If that's what you want to believe, then I can't change your mind," he said.

"And if you want to believe that me going on this trip means I'm going to betray you the way she did, then you do that." She grabbed her purse off the couch. "I think I'll spend the night at home tonight." Then she left.

Chapter 15

The town council chamber was filled to capacity. A hum of excitement filled the room from the multiple people waiting for the meeting to start. The waste-water provider was answering several tough questions the council posed to it based on the letter and comments submitted by the River Watchers before they gave any approvals for local permits.

"I think the council may deny this," Debra said after she and Danielle finished talking to a few of the residents of Crescent Acres. Since the council meeting was at six o'clock many of the residents had come out in support.

"I hope so. We've brought enough attention to the issue. There are a lot more people interested in protecting the river than there were before."

Thanks in a large part to Jacobe. The times he'd brought up the River Watchers, their website and social media accounts received a huge jump in hits. He may not have actively campaigned against the permit, but his knowledge of the subject when asked helped. The full council chambers was proof of that.

Danielle scanned the room again though the effort was useless. She would know if Jacobe was there. The buzz of conversation would have increased by now. She hadn't spoken to him privately since the argument. She still went to the semifinal games that were local. As Debra said, "Why waste good tickets?" He acknowledged her presence at least, but he didn't ask her to wait for him and hadn't asked her to attend the away games. Pain and anger were a constant clash inside her. He had said he trusted her, trusted her to *know better*.

A man and woman entered the council chambers. Hot, uncomfortable tingles rushed across her skin. "I don't believe it."

Debra looked up. "What's wrong?"

"My parents are here." They spotted her a second later. With hesitant smiles, they walked from the door of the chambers and over to her and Debra. Her mom had cut her hair, and her dad had more gray at his temples than before. The changes were a reminder that she hadn't seen them in a year.

"Mom, Dad, what are you doing here?"

Adele's smile appeared confident, but her eyes were uncertain. "Tonight's a big night for you. We missed the cleanup and the gala. We decided to come to the council meeting to show our support."

Debra touched Danielle's elbow. "I'm going to go sit down." Her smile was encouraging before she walked away.

Danielle focused back on her parents, shock and happiness swirling in her like a whirlpool. "You didn't have to do that. I could have come home this weekend and let you know how things went."

Her dad nodded. "You can still come home this weekend, or next. It's come to our attention that we've been too busy for our own daughter. That's about to change."

Danielle stepped forward, and took her mom's hand in one of hers and her dad's hand in the other. "I'm sorry I said that. Mom called on a bad day and I overreacted. I understand the work you two do is important."

"You're right," Adele said. "Our work in the community is important, but so are you. What you said made both of us realize that we don't always act that way. You were always so self-assured, so confident, we didn't think you needed our extra attention."

"I'll always need my parents," she said softly.

Her dad squeezed her hand. "We'll always be there to give it to you."

The intensity of the hum in the chambers increased. Awareness prickled the back of Danielle's neck. Jacobe was there. The thought passed a second before she glanced to the back of the room. His eyes were already on her. She gasped. He hadn't come alone. Will, Isiah, Kevin and other members of the team were there as well, and signing the paper to speak against the permit.

Her parents swiveled to see what the commotion was about. Adele looked back at Danielle. "Are you and he still dating?"

"We're cool," Danielle answered.

Her dad's brows drew together. "What does that mean?"

If only she had the answer to that. "Nothing. We're still dating, but it's not serious." That was the only answer she could think of that wouldn't have her dad bucking up overprotectively and her mom scowling at Jacobe.

Even though Jacobe and the rest of the team smiled and stopped to greet fans, it was clear he was making his way to her. She glanced across the room to where Debra, Mason and Patricia were all wearing victory grins. Danielle felt similar. This had to help their end.

She looked back at Jacobe and committed everything about him to memory, sure that soon she wouldn't even be able to say they were dating but not serious. His shoulders seemed broader, more powerful beneath a dark V-necked T-shirt and black blazer, his legs impossibly longer in dark slacks.

"You came," she said, when he made his way to her side. The rest of the team found seats in the chambers. "And you brought company."

"Of course I came. I would only have missed this for a game." He pointed to the rest of his team. "They just followed me." He looked at her parents.

Danielle quickly did the introductions. Jacobe's eyes widened. "I'm happy to meet you. Danielle has told me about the work you do in the community. It's admirable."

Her parents looked both proud and sheepish. "We're hoping to get more involved with Danielle's work."

The council members entered the chamber. Danielle led her parents and Jacobe to the seats in the front that Debra had saved for them. The council members quickly noticed the members from the Gators and smiled and waved their greetings. Everyone around here was an even bigger Gator fan now that the team had done so well in the play-offs.

The council meeting progressed quickly through the opening pledge of allegiance and as resolutions passed from the various members of the community. To Danielle's surprise, the chairman requested a change in the agenda to move the vote on the Clear Water permit up in the agenda. Danielle shifted in her seat and glanced at the agenda. He moved it ahead of the opportunity for citizens to speak. She gave Debra a wary look.

"What's this?" she whispered.

Debra shrugged. "I don't know and I don't like it."

Neither did Danielle. The council approved the change and then went straight into the vote.

Liberty sat forward in her chair and tilted the microphone forward. "As we can see from the turnout here today, including that from the members of our championship Gators team, this is an important issue. The council members have already discussed the seriousness of the outcome and have taken into consideration the multitude of phone calls, emails, and messages left by the community. Please remember that as we make our votes."

Danielle held her breath as she waited for each member to vote for or against the proposal. When the proposal passed unanimously to deny the local permit, even though Liberty's yes was less than enthusiastic, she nearly bounced out of her seat and yelped her joy. Not getting the local permit would go a long way to the ultimate denial of the state permit.

After the council meeting ended, there were a lot of congratulations and handshakes. The council members came over to Jacobe to thank him for bringing their attention to the issue.

"Great job, Danielle," her dad said when they were standing outside of the council chambers an hour later. It had taken that long for most of the crowd and residents to clear out.

"Thanks, but this is just the beginning. I've still got to work to make sure the state denies their permit. Clear Water needs to shut down, not put in patchworks that will do more harm than good. The state knows it."

Pride filled her mom's eyes and she hugged Danielle tight. "I love you, Danielle. And I'm so proud of you."

Tears burned the back of Danielle's eyes. She'd known her parents loved her, but hearing them say that and having them here was ten times better than having the feeling as a vague belief she kept telling herself.

Jacobe came over after her parents said goodbye and walked to their car. "Can I give you a ride home?"

"How do you know I need a ride?"

"Debra let it slip."

She'd have to remind Debra to butt out. They had ridden together to the council meeting. Danielle wanted to be petty and ask if he was sure he wanted to give her a ride, except her need to be alone with him again burned away any petty feelings she had. She missed him. "I'd like that."

"You're victorious," Jacobe said once they were seated in his car.

"Thanks to you."

"I'm only a part of it. I got the attention your way, but you're the one who did all of the talking to convince me, the council and the public to support the measure."

"Still, you got their attention. I appreciate that."

"Working with you all helped my reputation more than I expected. It's amazing how much people saw me as less the bad boy and more the good guy just because I helped out at your events."

Danielle had forgotten he was only helping out to improve his image and not because he had any real care for the environment. Jacobe gave back financially, but working with her was the only situation where he gave of his time. Obviously, he wouldn't have wanted to go with her on the Water for Kids trip. No wonder he'd scoffed when she'd mentioned she was going to ask him to go.

He shifted in his seat and glanced at her out of the corner of his eye. "I've done some thinking since the other night."

She clasped her hands in her lap and looked out of the window. "Oh, really? What have you come up with?"

"I was wrong, and I'm sorry."

Danielle's head whipped around. "What?"

"I'm sorry. I said I trusted you and I do. I think you should go to Malawi with Water for Kids."

"You want me to go?"

"If we weren't dating, would you have hesitated to say yes?"

She shook her head. "I wouldn't."

"I know. You should go. I know something like this will go a long way to bring attention to the River Watchers. Ultimately it'll help your goals here. Don't hold back your dreams because of me."

Words every woman wanted to hear from her man, but was he telling her not to hold back because he wasn't holding back his dream?

"If I go to Malawi, when I return will you be packing your bags for Phoenix?"

He shrugged. "I don't know, Danielle."

Pain tightened her chest. She faced the window again so he wouldn't see. His hand, warm and strong, covered hers on the armrest. "If I do go, that doesn't mean I want it to be the end of us, if that's what you're thinking. I can't ask you to drop everything in Jacksonville and move to another state. Well, I can, and I want to, but I won't pressure you into that decision."

He took his eyes off the road for a second to smile at her. "Not much anyway."

"Are you serious?"

"I am. I care about you, Danielle. I trust you. At the end of the summer, you'll be back and I'll know where I'm going to play next season. It'd be juvenile for us to break up now because of what might happen. Agreed?"

He cared about her. Not *love*, but again she knew that was a word he wouldn't throw out easily. Maybe they needed this. The heat between them had burned hot almost from the start, but heat didn't build a long-lasting relationship. Would absence make their heat burn hotter, or would she return to find he'd cooled off?

The thought pained her, but it was a very real possibility and one she'd rather face sooner rather than later. She didn't want to move to Phoenix, but maybe she would later. If they couldn't survive a summer apart, which was nothing in the scheme of things, how would they survive a long-distance relationship?

His hand squeezed hers. "What are you thinking about?"

"Everything you just said. Okay, I'll go. And I'll consider how we'll make things work when you move to Phoenix."

His nod was stiff. He lifted her hand to his lips and kissed the back. "Cool."

"Cool," she said. She was really starting to hate that word.

The atmosphere on the plane delivering the Jacksonville Gators back home after winning the last game of the semifinals and making their way to the finals was nothing less than exuberant. Singing, drinking, chanting and lively conversation filled first class and had spilled over into coach. Jacobe laughed and joined in with his teammates, but his heart wasn't really in it, and more than once he drifted away from the conversations to stare out the window.

"Jacobe," Isaiah called. "What are you doing when you get home?"

Jacobe turned away from the window to Isaiah in the seat next to him. Kevin sat in front of them and was currently on his knees facing backward to talk with them.

"I'm taking Danielle to the airport later." Surprisingly, he said that without any of the unsureness he felt inside.

Kevin shook his head. "You really want to send your girl off with her ex-boyfriend?"

"I'm not sending her off with her ex-boyfriend. She's going on a trip to bring water to those who need it."

"With her ex-boyfriend," Kevin said, raising an eyebrow. "You're not worried that he might try to cuddle up in her tent one night."

"No. Danielle isn't Christy." He kept telling himself this.

"She may not be like Christy, but that doesn't mean Luke won't push up on her."

Jacobe glanced at Isaiah next to him. "You think?"

Isaiah shrugged. "I'm not sure. I know he has a lot of good things to say about Danielle. I don't think he'll try and go there. He's all saved now, and breaking up relationships isn't his thing."

"He said that?" Jacobe asked.

Isaiah shrugged. "In so many words. I pressed him about his relationship with Danielle."

"Why did you do that?"

"Because you're my friend," Isaiah said without batting an eye. "I know Luke has been cool with us, but I don't work with him every day. I know that your history with Christy really messed with your head. If his plans were to get with Danielle I wanted to know so I could tell you."

Jacobe was struck speechless. He'd never really considered Isaiah and Kevin close friends. In a few sentences, Jacobe realized he'd been wrong not to. They had his back, were men he could trust. That felt nice. He hadn't understood how much he missed having friends he could count on. "I appreciate that, man."

"What did he say?" Kevin asked. "When you pressed him about Danielle?"

"Just that things didn't work out for them in college. In hindsight, he let them break up instead of trying to keep her. He doesn't blame her, and he's happy if she's happy. He wouldn't do anything to mess that up."

Jacobe raised a brow. "So he's not going to try to sneak into her tent, like Kevin says?"

Isaiah held up his hands and shrugged. "He said he'll see what happens. He's not trying to break up a relationship."

"But if she seemed *unhappy*, he'd step in to help make her happy."

Isaiah's look screamed, *Bull's-eye.* "I thought you needed to know that."

Kevin looked at Jacobe. "But you trust her?"

"I do." He did.

"Does she know you're in love with her?" Isaiah asked.

Kevin laughed. "In love? Normally, I'd say every man isn't ready to be saddled up like you are, Isaiah, but since I've got a G riding on this…" He looked at Jacobe. "Have you told her yet, so I can get my money?"

Jacobe slapped away Kevin's hand. "I care about her. And the bet was you got money if I proposed. I'm not there yet." Even though he had thought about being with Danielle forever.

"And you trust her," Isaiah said. "You don't trust women."

"Trusting and loving aren't the same," Jacobe argued.

Isaiah shrugged again. "I'm just saying, it wouldn't hurt to let her know how you feel before she gets on that plane."

Those words stuck with Jacobe for the rest of the flight and through his quick drive home to drop off his luggage before going to pick up Danielle. Not for the first time since she'd told him about her departure flight did he wish she wasn't leaving so soon after he got back in town. They'd barely have time to talk. Instead, he was sending her off on a trip where she did something great for the world and he stayed behind to play a game. For the first time ever, he wished they hadn't made the finals. If they hadn't, he would be able to go with her. Not send her on the plane with another guy.

Funny, for a guy whose game plan was "we'll see what happens."

He cared about her. He wanted to be with her. He didn't want any other guy to try to come between them. That wasn't the same as being in love with someone. If he was in love, he'd know it without any questions or hesitations.

He didn't trust Luke. Danielle knew Jacobe cared about her more than he had any other woman in years, but was that enough for her to tell Luke she was happy if he asked?

When he rang the doorbell, she swung the door open

just a few seconds later. Her eyes were bright with excitement and a grin covered her beautiful face.

"Congratulations!" She jumped into his arms and kissed his cheeks. "You're going to the finals! Aren't you excited?"

"Yes. More so about you all up in my arms like this." He squeezed her tight and kissed her. Holding her again felt good. He'd hated not having her in his arms when they'd fought.

"I'm so happy for you. You guys are going to win the championship. I know it."

He put her down and she turned to go into the living area. He followed, watching the sexy sway of her hips. She had on a pair of jeans and a green tank top that matched the Gators colors.

"I hope so."

"I wish I could be here to see it." She pulled a gold cardigan off the couch and slipped her arms into it.

"Yeah, so do I," he mumbled below his breath.

She turned a questioning glance his way. "What?"

He shook his head. "Nothing. Let's get you to the airport."

She talked about all the things Water for Kids had planned. She'd sent him a copy of the itinerary and promised to call. Her excitement about going on the trip she'd always dreamed about was palpable. Her enthusiasm only tightened the guilt in his stomach. All he wanted to do was turn around and ask her to stay.

"I wish I could wait with you at your gate," he said, after they'd checked her bags and were standing right before the security point. He pulled her against him and lowered his head to kiss her.

"I wish you could, too." Her arms tightened around his neck.

"Be safe and have fun." He started to let her go, then stopped. "Are you happy with me?"

She stopped smiling, and her eyes were serious when they met his. "Jacobe, I love you."

His heart dribbled against this ribs like an eight-ton basketball. He felt hot and cold. Free and trapped. Happy and uncertain. She loved him.

"Danielle, I…"

She pulled his head down and kissed him softly. "Don't say it just because I did. I just wanted to tell you before I left." She kissed him again. "I'll call you when I can."

Then she was out of his arms. In a daze, he watched her go through the security checkpoint before getting lost in the crowd. Danielle loved him, and he'd let her go without saying anything back.

Chapter 16

They'd won.

Jacobe stood in the middle of the court staring at the final score and the 00:00 time on the scoreboard, but the victory hadn't sunk in. The Jacksonville Gators were the league champions!

A second after that thought took hold, he grinned and was swarmed by people. His teammates, the media, members of the other team—everyone—were in the middle of the court. Congratulations went around, hands were shaken and microphones were stuck in his face, followed by questions of how he planned to celebrate this victory. His eyes kept going to the seats behind the bench.

He was happy. Ecstatic! Not only had the team that hadn't been predicted to win won, but they'd swept the series entirely. He was at the height of his career. On top of the world.

Why wasn't he more…happy?

"You cool, man?" Isaiah asked after they'd finished postgame interviews and were heading to the Suite to celebrate.

Jacobe nodded. "Yeah, I'm good."

"All right, because we are about to get crazy tonight." Isaiah slapped him on the back.

"You're getting crazy? Mr. Calm, Cool and Collected?"

"Man, we just swept the finals. I'm getting crazy. This is a dream come true. I just hope we can do the same thing next year."

"Yeah, me too." He meant it.

As they were leaving the auditorium, they passed fans lucky enough to make it back to the locker rooms. They shook hands and took selfies on the way out. Right before the door, a woman and young kid were waiting. Jacobe's heart tightened in his chest. Christy and Jake.

"You can just ignore her," Isaiah said.

Jacobe shook his head. "I can ignore Christy, but not Jake."

He walked over to them. Christy's smile was hesitant. Jake's was big and excited. He'd grown so much since Jacobe had seen him last. The three-year-old toddler now a tall seven-year-old. Jacobe studied Jake from head to toe. Even though DNA tests didn't lie, he couldn't help himself. He looked for any sign that the kid was his. There were none. Jake looked exactly like Martin.

Jake held out a basketball and a marker. "Hi, Mr. Jenkins. Can I have your autograph?"

The "Mr. Jenkins" hit Jacobe in the chest with the force of a heavyweight blow. Jacobe looked at Christy.

Her lips were pressed in a thin line. "He's a big fan," she said.

Jacobe looked back at Jake. The kid didn't know. Why didn't he know? Even though Martin insisted Jacobe stay away after discovering Jake's true paternity, there were dozens of pictures of him with Jacobe when he was a baby? He had to have seen them and asked his mom why was Jacobe in them. Unless Christy had gotten rid of the evidence. It would make sense. Hide the situation until Jake was old enough to understand.

Jake was pulling the ball back. Jacobe snapped out of his thoughts and smiled. "Sure." He took the ball and the pen. "What's your name?" The words hurt. Pretending he hadn't helped name him hurt.

"Jake Livingston." Martin's last name.

Jacobe was proud his hand didn't jerk as he wrote his autograph. He hoped his smile was friendly as he handed the ball back to Jake. "Here you go, Jake. Thanks for the support."

Jake stared at the signature, then grinned up at Jacobe. "Thank you. My dad's a basketball player. I hope to grow up and play just like he does."

Jacobe nodded. He couldn't stop himself from reaching out and rubbing the back of Jake's head. "Oh, yeah? You do that."

He glanced back at Christy. For the first time in years, she didn't look at him as if they could just be friends again. "I'm sorry, Jacobe," she said in a rough rush of words. She looked at Jake then back at Jacobe. Regret filled her eyes. "For everything."

He couldn't say they were okay. Could never say they'd be friends, or that he'd forget the way she and Martin had betrayed him. He couldn't continue to hold on to the anger or the hurt. "Apology accepted."

The encounter stayed on his mind as he drove to the Suite. None of the anger that typically consumed him when he thought about Christy and Jake filled him. He was ready to move on. He expected thoughts of Phoenix and future championships to fill his mind. It didn't.

His thoughts revolved around his friendship with Kevin, Isaiah, and Will. The pride of how their team had advanced to and swept the finals. He was considered an elite player here. The men on the team and Coach Simpson weren't just his colleagues—they were his family.

Then there was Danielle. She was here. That's why he couldn't be happier after the game. Danielle loved him, but she didn't want to move to Phoenix. She'd made her own connections here. She cared about the people and the places. She'd gotten him to do the same. Why on earth would he leave her? He loved her.

Why on earth had he sent her to Malawi without telling her?

Because you're a fool.

Jacobe swerved his car into an illegal U-turn at the next stoplight. Instead of going to the Suite he drove toward his home and pulled out his cell phone to call the airport. He had a flight to book.

Danielle sat in the passenger seat of a rugged Jeep while Luke drove them down a bumpy road to the next village. They'd mostly provided water filtration systems, but today, they were actually installing a well.

"I hear that the Gators won the finals," Luke said from the driver's seat.

Danielle turned to glance at him. "I know. I used the satellite computer at the last stop to check."

She'd talked to Jacobe a few days ago after they'd won the first two games in the series, but it was a quick call and he'd been tired after playing. She'd suspected then that they would win the series. They'd been doing so well she couldn't foresee how they couldn't win. She'd expected him to call and tell her.

"He didn't call to tell you?"

"I talked to him a few days ago."

"He doesn't call you every night."

"So?" she asked, her voice sharp.

Luke raised one of his hands. "Sorry, I didn't mean anything by that. I just noticed, that's all."

"Why would you notice something like that?"

"I would have called you every day."

Danielle sighed and turned back to the window. "We've been there before, Luke. You didn't call me every day."

"A mistake I've learned from."

"Are you calling your girlfriend every night then? I haven't paid attention to how often you get on the phone." A true statement. She'd spent most of her time here talking to the Water for Kids people. Her time with Luke had been limited.

"I'm not seeing anyone right now. If that's what you're asking."

"That's not what I'm asking."

"That's what it sounded like."

Danielle turned fully in her seat and narrowed her eyes on him. "Are you trying to make a point, Luke?"

"Are you happy with him?" He glanced at her again. "Seriously?"

"That's none of your business."

"Sounds like a no."

He sounded so sure her back went rigid. "Not only am I happy with him, I love him."

Luke's head swung around and he stared at her wide

eyed. The Jeep swerved to the right. He jerked it back in line with the train of vehicles in their party.

"You love him?"

"I do, and I think he feels the same."

Luke's brows went up. "You think?"

"Leave it alone." She turned back to the window, her face hot with anger and embarrassment. She sounded stupid. *I think he loves me.*

"Danielle, if he hasn't said he loves you, then you don't know for sure that's how he feels. You could just be making this up in your head."

"I'm not." She held up her hand to stop him from talking anymore. "Luke, we're friends. If you want us to remain that way, then stop talking. Stay out of my personal life."

Luke didn't say anything else for the remainder of the drive. Danielle stared out of the window, a multitude of thoughts swirling through her brain. They arrived at the next location thirty minutes later. She and Luke joined the rest of the group gathering around their guide's Jeep at the front of the caravan. Their guide had gone into the main building of the small town to find out about lodging before they unpacked all of their items.

The guide returned with a questioning look on his face. "They say someone from our group is already here." His eyes scanned the group. "I counted us all and no one left early or got lost."

"Are they sure it's someone from our group?" Luke asked.

"That's what the leader says. He said this guy came in yesterday and said he was with us."

"That sounds suspicious to me," Luke said. "Our trip isn't exactly a secret. It could be any wacko who knew we were coming here and is trying to get close to us."

"Apparently, the guy is out at the old well site now," the guide said. "He went there this morning. The villagers have already begun working on the irrigation trenches and he volunteered to help."

"Let's go see who this so-called volunteer is."

"I'll go with you," Danielle said.

Luke looked at her with concern. "Danielle, I'd prefer if you stayed here. We don't know anything about this guy. If he is crazy and things get rough, I'd rather you be away from any danger."

Danielle laughed. "I doubt a man who's helping villagers dig a trench would be dangerous. You said yourself one or two other celebrities wanted to volunteer but couldn't make it. Maybe it's one of them."

Luke sighed. "Fine, but stay behind me."

Danielle rolled her eyes. "I'm not some damsel in distress. I'll be fine."

"We'll go with you two," said one of the other football players from Luke's team.

Ten of them made their way to the old well site. If the volunteer was some crazy person, then they had nearly a ton of defensive linemen to answer to. The group of villagers digging the trench stopped as they noticed them approaching. They began talking excitedly and pointed to the people digging in the trenches. One man stood straight and cocked his head toward the villagers talking.

Danielle's breath caught in her throat. His back was turned, but she'd recognize that tall body and wide shoulders anywhere. When he turned to look at her, her heart danced. She grinned and took off running. Jacobe braced his arms on the side of the waist-deep trench and hauled himself out. He sprinted and reached her a few seconds later.

Danielle flung herself into his arms. "What are you doing here?"

"I'm dirty, Danielle," he said at the same time.

He was dirty. Filthy, actually. Dust and grime clung to his handsome face. She guessed his T-shirt was supposed to be white but was, instead, a rust color that matched the dirt on his jeans. She recognized them as an expensive pair that had never been made to wear during manual labor. He smelled like sweat and dirt. Beneath that the delicious musk that was all him.

"I don't care that you're dirty," she said. "Why are you here?"

"I'm digging a trench, woman. Can't you see?" He used his head to nod toward the trench.

"Don't be stupid. You just won the finals. Aren't you supposed to be going to Disneyland or working out the details of your transfer to Phoenix?"

"That's the thing—I'm not going to Phoenix."

Her heart jumped with excitement. "You aren't?"

"No. Jacksonville is home. The guys, coach, the city that I'm helping clean up—it's where I belong. Everything I want is there."

"Everything?"

His sexy grin made her body tingle all over. "Everything, including you. I should have said this before you left. I love you, Danielle. I shouldn't have let you leave without telling you how I feel."

Danielle wrapped her arms around his neck and squeezed him tight. "I love you, too, Jacobe. Even if you were going to Phoenix I would have wanted to make this work. Don't feel like you have to turn down the opportunity because of me."

"This is because of me. I've been afraid to trust people and to make a home for myself after what Christy did. Not anymore. I'm ready to make a new home with you—if you're ready to be mine forever."

She was so happy she could have exploded into a million pieces of stardust and it wouldn't have been enough. "I'm already yours forever. Only yours."

Epilogue

The sound of the ocean, along with the gentle sway of the hammock, and Jacobe's body curled up behind her, nearly lulled Danielle to sleep. Even being mostly naked except for the sheet wrapped around her, on a balcony in a villa in the French Riviera wasn't enough to keep her eyes open. Moonlight created shadows around them, she was thoroughly sated, completely happy, and absolutely lazy.

After leaving Malawi, Jacobe surprised her with a quick weekend in a villa along the French coastline. Tonight was their last night. She looked forward to getting back to work. Debra had kept her abreast of what was happening, and her parents were excited to see her. Well, maybe looking forward to wasn't the right phrase. Didn't dread was more suitable.

Jacobe tightened his hold around her. "I told you there is a definite perk to a vacation where all you do is have sex." His deep voice washed over her in the quiet night.

She smiled and snuggled closer into his warmth. "I wish it could last longer."

"I thought you were ready to go home."

"I miss my parents, and my friends," she said. "At the same time I never want to leave."

He kissed the top of her head. "Why?"

"Because I never want to forget how happy I am here with you."

"You won't. I'll make sure of it."

"Oh, really," she said in a low, pleased voice. "How are you going to do that?"

"By giving you something that will always remind you of tonight."

Danielle's eyes opened. Curiosity bubbled up inside of her. "You got me a gift?"

"Wait. I've got to get up." He slid her out of his embrace and got out of the hammock.

Danielle tightened the sheet around her chest and frowned. "Why? I liked laying here with you."

Jacobe grinned at her and wrapped the other sheet around his waist. "Just wait."

She let out a fake groan of annoyance. He went over to where his pants were folded over a chair. Danielle begrudgingly got up from her comfortable position to sit and let her legs hang off the side. Even though she wished he hadn't moved, she did enjoy the view of his muscular body in nothing but a sheet and moonlight.

Jacobe returned with a hand behind his back. He awkwardly lowered to one knee. The sheet around his waist hindered his movements. Danielle's throat constricted, and her heart danced.

"Danielle, will you do me the honor of marrying

me?" He brought his hand from around his back and opened a small black box that held a beautiful diamond ring.

Danielle sucked in a breath. Tears stung her eyes and happiness burst in her chest. "Yes!"

Jacobe got up and came to her. He took her hand in his and stared into her eyes. "Are you sure? I mean, I know this may seem sudden, but I love you, Danielle. I don't want anyone else, and I know I never will. I've wanted you since that first study session in college and nothing's changed. After all these years, I only want you more."

Tears slid down Danielle's face, but her smile couldn't be suppressed. Jacobe slid the ring on her finger then wiped away her happy tears. "Are *you* sure?" she asked. "Really sure. I love you, too, Jacobe. There's no one else for me, but you're going to be on the road. You're going to be giving up a lifestyle most men dream ab—"

He kissed her softly. "I'm completely sure. I've lived that lifestyle. I don't want do to that anymore. I want you with me at as many away games as you can make. There's no other woman I need by my side. In fact—" He leaned down and got his cell phone off the table near the hammock. "Hold up your hand."

She did and he took a picture of her with her hand up. The flash temporarily blinded her. After several blinks she watched him do something on his phone.

"What are you doing?"

"This." He held up the phone so she could see the screen. Her jaw dropped. He'd posted the picture online, thankfully of just her hand—diamond ring shining—next to her smiling face, with the caption: *She just made me the happiest man alive!!!*

Danielle laughed and snatched the phone from him. "I can't believe you did that."

He cupped the side of her face in his hand. "Let the world know I'm officially off the market. I've hid from relationships for too long. I won't hide this. I want everyone to know we're together. That I'll never leave you behind. That I love you."

Her heart filled with so much emotion, she couldn't speak. Tears came again. Jacobe leaned forward and kissed them away. Instantly her body responded. The masculine strength of his body pressed against hers, and she eased back in the hammock. His cell phone buzzed in her hand.

Danielle broke the kiss and looked at his phone. A text from Kevin popped up. Without her glasses, she squinted and read the message.

You owe me a G!!

"Why do you owe Kevin a thousand dollars?"

Jacobe grinned and looked at the message on the screen. He took the phone from her, which was now chiming with tons of responses to the picture. He silenced it before tossing the phone to the side. "Kevin told me from the start I was going to fall in love with you. He bet me. I lost."

"I would say I'm sorry," Danielle said grinning. She wrapped her arms around his neck.

"Don't." Jacobe pulled at her sheet until her body was naked beneath him. "That's a bet I'm happy to lose."

* * * * *

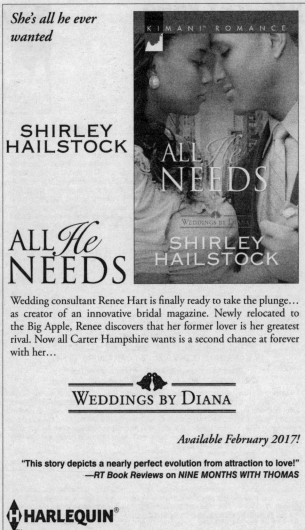

REQUEST YOUR FREE BOOKS!

2 FREE NOVELS
PLUS 2 FREE GIFTS!

KIMANI ™
ROMANCE

Love's ultimate destination!

Turn your love of reading into
rewards you'll love with

Harlequin My Rewards

**Join for FREE today at
www.HarlequinMyRewards.com**

Earn **FREE BOOKS** of your choice.

Experience **EXCLUSIVE OFFERS** and contests.

Enjoy **BOOK RECOMMENDATIONS**
selected just for you.

PLUS! Sign up now
and get **500** points
right away!

Earn
FREE
REWARDS
HarlequinMyRewards.com
Join
Today!

MYR16R

*Liam Westbrook didn't make his way to the top playing
it safe. So when the fast-living British bachelor spies an
exotic beauty under a smoldering North Carolina moon,
he makes a scandalous proposal. Divorced single mother
Maya Alvarez does something totally out of character. She
accepts an invitation that leads to a hot summer fling with
a seductive stranger. When Maya must return to the real
world, will Liam and their pleasure-fueled fantasy end up
as only an affair to remember?*

Read on for a sneak peek at
PLAYING WITH DESIRE,
the first exciting installment in author Reese Ryan's
***PLEASURE COVE** series!*

"Mr. Westbrook, I'll seat you now." The hostess approached
Hot Suit Guy with a menu.

"That's our table, love." The man stood, extending his
hand to her.

Her eyes traveled up the sleeve of his expensive suit.
Definitely athletic cut.

The man was tall, and even more handsome upon closer
inspection. Michael Ealy meets Adam Levine handsome.

Her heart beat a little faster and a jolt of electricity
traveled the length of her spine. She shuddered inwardly.
Handsome and charming, and he damn well knew it.

A man like that is bad news.

She had two kids and a divorce decree to prove it. It would be safer to pass on the invitation. And she intended to, because that was just what she did. She made sensible choices. Played it safe. But the man's expectant grin taunted her. Dared her to venture beyond the cozy cocoon of her safe and predictable life.

He's being a gentleman. Why not let him?

Maya placed her hand in his and let him pull her to her feet. Heat radiated up her arm from the warmth of his hand on hers. His clean scent—like freshly scrubbed man, new leather and sin—was captivating.

Maybe sin didn't have a scent, per se. But if it did, it would smell like him, with his mischievous smile and eyes so dark and intense they caused a flutter in her belly whenever she looked into them.

She tucked her hand into the bend of his elbow as he followed the hostess to their table. Maya concentrated on putting one foot in front of the other. The simple feat required all of her concentration.

"Thank you." The words tumbled from her lips the second the hostess left them alone. "It was kind of you to come to my rescue, but I doubt dinner with a random stranger was your plan for tonight. I'll order something to go from the bar and let you get back to your evening." The inflection at the end of the phrase indicated it was a question. She hadn't intended it to be. The thinking part of her brain clearly wasn't the part of her body in control at the moment.

His dark eyes glinted in the candlelight. "My motives aren't as altruistic as you might imagine. The opportunity to dine with a beautiful woman presented itself, so I seized it. I'd much prefer your company to eating alone."

Don't miss PLAYING WITH DESIRE
by Reese Ryan, available March 2017
wherever Harlequin® Kimani Romance™
books and ebooks are sold.